Dead Deutsch
a Jud Carson mystery

by John M. Spafford

Dead Deutsch
a Jud Carson mystery

by John M. Spafford

Dedication:

To the men and women who successfully waged
the Cold War in Central Europe – and, especially,
to my colleagues at
"The KUF"

Spaff

Appreciation:

*With heart-felt thanks to Peggy, Sean,
Colm, "Daisy"
- and to Paula, wherever you may be...*

Preface:

After *Dead Duck* I knew that I was done with Jerome Carstead and his hard-hitting detective Jud Carson. I had written *Duck* in the middle of a snow storm in Germany. Readers and friends (and readers who became friends – even a few friends who became readers) asked me when the next one was coming out. I told them the truth – never. It's done. Moving on.

Like hell I was.

Because then I went back to Germany. From Tegel Airport I took the metro from the old West through the old East without seeing a single Soviet guard. I saw my old friend Checkpoint Charlie, now manned with German actors playing American G.I.s, and walked through the Brandenburg Gate just like Montgomery Clift in *The Big Lift*, which is a great film, by the way.

So here I was with a good friend re-visiting Berlin (now without the 'West' appellation) when Jud Carson snuck up behind me on the trolley car. He's like that – the sneaky bastard. In his typical style he didn't intrude on all of my moments – just enough to annoy me until I listened to the tale and jotted down some notes in a notebook that I picked up in Potsdam, Germany (now without the 'East" appellation). It didn't take long to listen. Not much longer to bang out the text. The critics will assure you that they can tell that last statement is a fact.

Most of the tale told in this tiny tome is made up.

But only most of it.

All the best,

John M. Spafford

West Berlin

He keeps the wire stretched tight on the autobahn –
     Runs from Helmstedt to West Berlin
They look his papers over at Check Point Alpha –
     And they let him in
He salutes the Soviet guard at the border –
     Ignores the East German later on
He's heading for the wall where the sun comes up –
     In West Berlin

She wakes up with her hair in a mess
     And wonders, "Was last night's named 'Jim'?"
She wonders how she made it home all –
     And she wonders where she's been
Then going out to the balcony
     She tries to make sense of it all
And the sun is slowly coming up
     from the wall –
     And over West Berlin

And all across the city
     The people are just trying to be
Trying to find a normal life –
     In a city half in captivity
To forget about the Warsaw Pact
     Or the need for their American 'friends'
But it's hard to think about anything else –
     When you're in West Berlin

The radio is tuned to the milit'ry station –
     The weather should be fair
The Russians are calling the Americans names
     If anybody cares
And late last night somebody died

In the flame of East German guns
Tried to make it through the wall 'fore the came up –
And into West Berlin

She keeps her secrets –
Says that she waited for him
He knows she's lying – lets it go –
'Cause it doesn't matter where she's been
And somebody's digging tunnels –
In spite of those who want to keep them in
Trying to make it through the wall
'fore the sun comes up –
And out of East Berlin

Out of East Berlin –
Out of East Berlin
And into
West Berlin

Chapter One

Notebook 24, Entry 14

"All of the characters in this tale are real. The people that they're based on are all fictitious. Figure it out for yourself."

- *When the Clock Strikes Dead*
Jud Carson, P.I.

*****

Excerpt, Daily Read File:
Tuesday, 2 May 1989
BBC Monitoring/FBIS

(Budapest, Hungary) Government announces dismantling of 240 km (150 mile) barbed-wire fence along Austrian border.

*****

Florian Schumann narrowed his eyes and studied the form that was making its way toward him across the wide lawn of his country house on the outskirts of Berlin. His seventy-odd years of life had robbed him of his once acute vision and his ego made him rebel against using the glasses that had been prescribed years before. He would relent in private to study the reports if necessary, but he preferred to listen to his secretary read to him while he, closed eyed and leaning back in his leather chair, or even reclining on the sofa in his office, listened, questioned and considered.

The figure had reached the periphery of Schumann's vision; it was a woman – a woman in a business-length maroon skirt and a matching silk blouse. Paula Layman came into focus and the old man smiled. She returned his smile and gave him a short wave. The breeze pressed against her body, forming the silk of her blouse to full breasts, the linen of her skirt to lush hips. She was no longer a twenty-something, but she didn't appear to be a thirty-something either. She had managed to cheat time of a decade for years. And, while her appearance made her look no older than her mid-twenties, her attitude and energy could sometimes make her seem to be in her teens.

Her youthfulness often became a trap for those who mistook her attitude with her ability. Schumann had originally interviewed and hired her as a personal assistant because of her impressive resume and astute grasp of the scope and delicacy of his responsibilities to the German government. She was especially well-informed because, as a former member of the U.S. Air Force intelligence unit stationed in Berlin, she knew the language and processes of her former employer. It was no secret that she had hung up her uniform under duress.

While the break-up was inevitable, it had been a one-way street. She had loved the military more than it loved her. Still, there was no bitterness and no one even suggested that she might betray her allegiance to her country in favor of her new boss.

In the few months that she had been with Schumann, he had admired her chameleon-like ability to blend into the background at times and at others to forcefully make her presence known. Even then her quick, quirky smile and flashing blue eyes could disarm business or government representatives despite her often stress-inducing questions, comments and observations.

However much he admired her skills as a sometimes silent witness, sometimes foil and sometimes strong-arm, the elderly statesman had quickly come under the sway of her more intimate charms. The age and social differences between them did not seem to be even noticed by her. He was a man and she a woman. The development of their relationship, both professionally and personally, had been so natural and organic that, although he could not say that it had happened without his realizing it, it had not felt contrived or pressured. He had always felt that he was in control and that he could have changed to direction of their association if he chose. It was just that Paula made it so easy to not make that change.

It had seemed inevitable that their work together would lead to dinners and that the dinners would lead to laughter, and that the laughter would lead, in turn, to kisses.

She had been his equal, or even the senior member of the pair from the moment that she had allowed him to put his arms around her. When he had told her, afterward, that he was married she had laughed, patted his naked thigh and sat up in his bed. He wished that she had not turned to put her feet on the floor. If she had turned toward him he would have been able to watch the sheet cascade away from her full breasts and reveal the large, blush-colored nipples and the delicate, dusky rose of the areolas that surrounded them. Paula Layman made him feel young again. And she made him glad that he had lived long enough to be able to appreciate a woman like her.

"I know you're married," she had said, standing and making her way across the thick carpet to the bathroom. "It doesn't seem to have slowed you down!" She had turned, half-closed the door, and a moment later he had heard the shower running.

He pulled his thoughts back to the present and tried to ignore the stirring that he felt at both the woman's virtual presence in his memory and her actual presence as she stopped in front of him, hands resting on the table between them. Her smile made the day even brighter.

"I think we have some good news," she said.

"Good news?" he asked.

"Make that 'very good news'," she said.

"Then you will have to sit and tell me all about it," he said. He lifted the telephone receiver and, after a few seconds asked for a second coffee service to be brought out.

"I could use some 'very good news'," Schumann said, replacing the handset.

"You have to hold onto something when I tell you this." Paula tossed her head from side to side, letting the movement and the breeze push the reddish-brown hair from across her face. "It seems that you may have friends in very strange places, *Herr* Schumann."

"How strange, *Fraulein* Layman?"

She beamed at him and winked. "How about

Rusche and Normannen Streets? Strange enough for you?"

*****

Notebook 24, Entry 15

"Sure, the gap between what is and what a client comes to me for is generally only slightly wider than the Grand Canyon. And it's generally only a little less than impossible to being something that they are going to step across to getting.

"I've been measuring that gap for clients who thought that they could walk on air for long enough to be able to spot just how many have a chance of putting my talents to work and getting everything that they want for a pile of nothing in return. I can count their number comfortably on no fingers of either hand.

"That doesn't stop the fairly steady stream of men and women – mostly women – who want me to solve their problems in a matter of minutes armed with nothing but a few bucks and a lot of lies. And knowing it doesn't stop me from taking the cases, spending the cash and pretending that I believe the lies that they tell me – while they pretend I don't know that nearly everything that comes out of their mouths is lies.

"Most of what I deal with is agony and greed and treachery and pettiness – and the first casualty of those – just as in war – is truth.

"I'm going to tell enough lies in this version of the truth to make it tough, if not impossible, to hang a rap on me for telling tales out of school."

-   *When the Clock Strikes Dead*
Jud Carson, P.I.

*****

Excerpt, Daily Read File:
Tuesday, 19 August 1989
BBC Monitoring/FBIS

(Warsaw, Poland) In a stunning move
today, Wojciech Jaruzelski, the Polish
president, has nominated the Solidarity
Union activist Tadeusz Mazowiecki to be
the country's new Prime Minister. Mr.
Mazowiecki will be the first non-
communist in such a position of power
for the last 42 years.

A peace demonstration, called by
organizers Otto von Habsburg and Imre
Pozsgay as 'The Pan-European Picnic'
was held near the town of Sopron, on
the Austrian-Hungarian border. Hundreds
of East Germans have fled unhindered,
and, reportedly even assisted by,
unarmed Hungarian border guards into
Austria.

This seems to echo the activities of 27
June when Alois Mock, the Austrian
foreign minister, and Gyula Horn,
foreign minister of Hungary, cut
through the border fence near the site

of today's events.

On 2 May Hungary began to dismantle and
remove border surveillance equipment
and installations on its common border
with Austria.

*****

Gwen (she preferred 'Gwendolyn' but few
people called her that) Dean opened the glass doors
that led out onto the small balcony of her San
Francisco apartment and let the chill of the early
morning breeze wash over her. Her breath quickened
and her small nipples stiffened beneath the
handkerchief material of her bra. She stretched and
smiled and caressed the flat plane of her stomach,
letting her fingers brush against the lace stitched to
the top of her pink panties. Today was the day, she
thought. She turned, padded barefoot across the oak
hardwood floor and into the small bathroom, relieved
herself, washed her hands and then her face, then
made her way into the kitchen where she filled the tea
kettle and set it to boil.

She opened the tea tin on the counter and
removed a bag tagged 'Celestial Seasonings' and put
it in her grandmother's primrose-patterned tea cup,
draping the string over the side and letting it rest on
the matching saucer. While the water heated she sat
at the table, crossed her slim legs and hummed a
tune. But most of all she thought about the phone call
that she had received the night before from the
concierge, Brian.

He was back, Brian had told her. Yes, he was

alone. There was nothing new there, he was always alone. Well, she intended to do something about that. He might not be a Pulitzer Prize winner but he was an author, and, according to people who would know, successful enough to be quite comfortable. Gwendolyn saw no reason why she shouldn't be comfortable, too. And if that meant having to engineer a relationship with the shy man who ducked his head each time that she saw him, what of it? Men engineered relationships all the time. They arranged to 'accidently' meet the objects of their desires. They contrived excuses to speak and to spend time together.

Besides, she had actually read one of his books, well, she admitted to herself, most of part of one. But it was pretty good. And, more importantly, she thought, it wasn't as if she intended to ask him for money. She was prepared to enter into a relationship with him. One that was mutually beneficial. If he decided to help her financially, well, he was a grown man, after all. And, if he did seem rather pedestrian for her tastes, so what? This was San Francisco. People's lives here tended to have as many curves as the streets that they travelled.

God knows my last few choices haven't worked out too well, she thought as the kettle began to whistle. Without rising she reached out, turned off the stove and lifted the kettle. After filling her cup she set the kettle on the wooden trivet and sniffed the tea as it began to brew.

Huey, her last beau, had been fired for using his position to coerce his way into the beds of the women he was supposed to be supervising. But, he assured her, it wasn't true. Still, she had ended the relationship immediately. Well, immediately after he had helped her, as he had already promised, with the month's rent. And, as bad as that situation had been, it had been much better than the one that gone before it. Gwendolyn Dean shuddered at that memory.

She brought her thoughts back to the moment. This would take some doing, she knew. But she could arrange 'accidental' run-ins as well as any man. And she could bring even the most shy of men to the point of boldness. She just had to let them know who she wanted them to think was the boss, she smiled.

She studied the color of her tea and judged it done steeping. She lifted the bag by its string and laid it on the edge of the saucer before picking up the cup by its delicate handle and sipping. Just right, Gwendolyn Dean thought.

*****

Notebook 24, Entry 16

"It's just a helluva damned no-good thing," Stu Allgood said to no one in particular.

"Your bangtail come in last again?" I asked.

"I had crossed the lobby of my hotel of residence and come up on the house detective's blind side. The doctor had done a good job. Except for a lack of luster the glass eye matched up pretty well and most people didn't twig unless he forgot to lift the shade on that side.

"I wish it was just that," Stu said. "I wish to hell-and-a-half that I never got another winner rather than this."

"I studied him and then shook my head. "So are you going to let me in on the tragedy?" I asked at last. "Or do I have to wait to read about it in the rags?"

"You mean to tell me that an in-the-know guy like you isn't already on the inside of this?" He turned on me and shook his head. "I would have thought that you would know before me! A helluva-damned thing like this!"

"Stu, tell me what is going on."

"Danny Granger," he said simply. "He's dead. Took three in the chest in his very own damned living room."

"My gut turned over. Granger and I had known each other for a lot of years. A few years older than me, he had tossed me occasional work when I was still a green op. He'd done that for a lot of guys, just to keep us in the business and off of the soup or factory line.

"Now aint that a helluva damned no-good thing?" Stu asked.

"My lights dimmed for an instant. Then I squared my shoulders and turned away. "Yeah," I said. "It's a helluva damned no-good thing." I started across the lobby toward the elevator on the far wall.

"She's up there waiting for you," Stu said from behind me.

"I turned. "Who is?"

"Dixie," he said. "I told her she could wait for you up there."

"A couple of minutes later I was walking from the elevator toward Dixie LaBlanc, already in widow's black, sitting on the small couch in the sitting room of the fifth floor.

"I'm sorry – " I started but Dixie waived my

sympathy off.

"Danny always said to make sure that you got – this – stuff. I found some more and just put it in – whatever was on his desk – I didn't want the dicks going through his things." There was a sniffle that told me tears were close to the surface.

"Was Danny onto something?" I asked. I found that I was avoiding looking at the box. It was like looking into his grave and I wasn't ready to do that just yet.

"Dixie shrugged. "Dan was always onto something. You know that."

"I nodded. "What about the cops?" I pursued. "Do they have anything?"

"Not much. I was doing a show, so it was just Dan and the killer at our place. A neighbor called the cops when he heard the shots."

"See anything?"

"She shook her head. "Probably hiding in a closet."

"At least he called," I offered.

"Yeah, at least. Could of maybe come and – tried –
"

"Hey, Dix," I said, "from what I hear, it was delivered before he knew it was in the mail."

"I had more questions but I just couldn't bring myself to ask them.

"Dixie, why don't you come down to my place and we can talk?" I offered. "I've got some 12-year-old Scotch that needs to express itself." I wasn't all that comfortable being around a dead colleague's squeeze so soon after he had had his ticket punched, but I couldn't just say 'Thanks for coming by' and leave it at that, either. I owed Dixie more than that. And I sure as hell owed Danny Granger more than that.

"But I didn't have to worry. With a shrug Dixie had turned and started for the elevator. "Too bad you didn't make that offer when Danny was still alive," she said. "We could have had some laughs."

"She walked away and made it count but only in the 'could-have-been' way that means it sure as hell doesn't have a chance of being anymore. I had to admit that I could admire the packaging even though I wouldn't want to unwrap it. Every vice has a limit and I was pretty sure that I had learned most of mine a long time ago.

"I picked up the box and made my way to my rooms. I put it on the kitchen counter and went into the living room. I needed a stiff drink before I started going through Danny's life. I passed up the 12-year-old that was reserved for special guests. The cheap, raw stuff would suit the moment better.

"Without the box obscuring my view I could see the small ivory-colored envelope that had been slipped under my door sometime earlier. I picked it up and poured my drink, slammed it down and poured another before breaking the seal. Inside was a note that named a time and place. I figured it must be from someone who shared my convictions because the sender had included a dollar sign at the bottom."

\-   *When the Clock Strikes Dead*
Jud Carson, P.I.

*****

Gwendolyn Dean dropped the magazine that she had been holding and not reading onto the glass and granite end table beside her and stood up. She waited until he had pushed the 'Up' elevator button before making her way across the lobby to stand just behind Jerome.

"Hey!" she said, "Aren't you the famous writer who lives in our building?"

Jerome turned his head slightly, brought his right foot back and turned to face her with a guarded expression. "I don't think that we have met," he said.

"I'm Gwen, Gwendolyn, really, Dean," she said, offering her hand.

"Pleased to meet you," Jerome answered. "I'm – "

"Oh, you don't have to tell me!" Gwendolyn assured him. "Everyone knows who you are!"

Jerome felt his right cheek tick. "You are very kind," he said.

The bell rang and the elevator doors opened. "Going up?" he asked. When she nodded he gestured slightly and moved aside a few inches more to allow her to enter first.

Inside he turned to her again, "What floor?"

"Three," Gwendolyn replied. She moved a bit closer to him and smiled.

"I'm just below you," he said, pushing the two buttons.

"Hmmm…" Gwendolyn murmured.

When he did not respond she moved around to face him more directly. "I bet you hear this all the time," she began, "but, since you write novels – well –

is it hard?"

"Not if you settle for the way that I do it," he said, trying to make his response sound light-hearted and realizing that he had failed.

The elevator climbed, came to a stop and the doors slid open. Jerome took a step out and realized that his companion was joining him. He looked at the floor indicator on the elevator car and the one in the hallway: Two. "I think you need to go up one more floor," he said.

Gwendolyn stepped a bit closer. "Well, if you don't mind, I've never seen a real writer's place. Or you could come up to my apartment. I have some wonderful tea I could brew."

Jerome studied her for a long moment. At last she laughed, a bit nervously. "You're looking at me as if I think you owe me money! I just want to – well – talk. But, if you're busy – "

"No," Jerome cut her off. "It's not that – I just, well, I wasn't expecting this."

"I thought writers were always expecting the unexpected," Gwendolyn said.

"Characters expect the unexpected," Jerome corrected. "Writers are just people. People can be surprised." He gestured toward the elevator and they stepped back inside the brass-accented and mahogany-paneled car. He pushed the button for Gwendolyn's floor. "In this case," he went on, "very pleasantly surprised."

Gwendolyn Dean gave him her best coy expression.

When the elevator stopped again and the doors had opened she led him to the left, stopping at her door and handing him the key.

"Kind of an old-fashioned gesture," he remarked, turning the lock and stepping back.

"Well, I am a kind of old-fashioned girl," she said. She brushed past him, took the key back and dropped it on the mock Queen Anne table in the foyer. "Make yourself comfortable," she said, breezing into the kitchen and putting the kettle on the burner.

Jerome took in the small but inviting room. Turquoise and corals were used sparingly but effectively; Gwendolyn Dean might not have much money, but she seemed to have good taste. The sheers were open and the light streamed in from the small balcony and reflected off of the polished wood floors.

To his right the open door revealed the bedroom. The bed with its lace comforter dominated his view. The bed had been made but a navy blue skirt, topped with a pale yellow bra and matching panty was in clear view on the side nearest the door. The arrangement looked as accidental as a bank robbery, he thought.

Beyond the bed was a vanity and when he glanced at it he saw his own reflection, and, behind him, standing in the kitchen doorway watching him, Gwendolyn Dean. Her arms were folded below her breasts and she was leaning comfortably, one hip thrust out against the door-frame. She still wore a bit of her smile.

He turned and walked toward the small sofa, waited until she had joined him before sitting, and made room for her when she made her intent obvious.

"Is it lonely?" she asked.

"What?"

"Being a writer – it would seem like it would be lonely. Is it?"

Jerome nodded slightly. "Sometimes." His discomfort was apparent.

"But it gets easier, right?"

He shook his head. "Look, I don't profess to be anything important. I started writing because I didn't want to bag groceries to get through college. I found out that I could put stories together and it beat working."

"Yeah, but you're good at it," she said.

"I'm good *enough* at it," he countered.

"What's your process?"

Jerome thought for a few seconds, then, just as he was about to speak, the tea kettle whistle began to sound and Gwendolyn held up the index finger of her right hand. "Just a sec," she said, bounding up and dashing into the kitchen.

"How do you like yours?" she called.

"Just plain," he said.

A moment later she had returned with a tray laden with cups, saucers, spoons, a bowl of sugar – real sugar, he noted – and some lemon slices. When they had the cups in hand she flashed him her smile again. "Okay," she said, "time in – you were saying?"

"Good tea," Jerome said. Then, "Look, I only know a few things about writing."

"Like what?"

"Well," he squinted as though trying to remember something. "Well, let's see. Write fast, edit slow. Know where to begin, what not to put in, and when to end."

"That covers a lot of territory!" Gwendolyn said.

"Yeah, I guess," Jerome conceded. He sipped

his tea before going on. "You can begin earlier or later – but never at the beginning. You can put in less and make more of it. And you always have to end sooner."

"That's it?" she asked.

"That's it *for me*," he said.

They drank their tea in silence for a moment. "You have a lovely apartment," he said at last.

"You are quite a gentleman," Gwendolyn answered.

"Well, I try to be appropriate," he said.

"I think that I would like to see what happens when you aren't so appropriate," Gwendolyn said softly, bringing her tea cup to her lips again.

A half hour later Gwendolyn walked him to the door and held it for him as he stepped into the hallway.

"We'll have to do this more often," she said.

"I have to admit," he said, "you remind me of someone that I would like to get to know better. I hope that that isn't too inappropriate."

"Just inappropriate enough," she said. "For a start, anyway."

*****

Excerpt, Daily Read File:
Tuesday, 23 August 1989
BBC Monitoring/FBIS

(Vilnius, Lithuania) On the 50th anniversary of the Molotov-Ribbentrop Pact that divided Eastern Europe into spheres of influence to be governed by Nazi Germany or its then-ally, the

Soviet Union, millions of Estonians, Latvians, and Lithuanians have joined hands to form a human chain they call the 'Baltic Way' and stretching 600 km in a call for their freedom and democratic reforms.

(Budapest, Hungary) In a move that builds on the activities that began on 2 May of this year, the government of Hungary has removed all border restrictions with its Western-allied neighbor, Austria.

Chapter Two

Gwendolyn Dean eased back into the door frame of *The Colonnades* apartment building and seemed to mold herself to it. Her small, shapely hands rested on the polished oak and reminded Jerome of those of saints painted by renaissance masters. Her head was tilted slightly down but her eyes, bright blue and seemingly attentive to his every movement or mood, invited him to interrupt his progress through the building in order to spend time with her. The brass plaque beside her – 891 Post Street – sent a starburst that seemed too contrived to be accidental and, at the same time, completely natural.

He could feel the change in his breathing as he nodded to her and silently cursed himself for smiling too quickly and too openly.

She's so beautiful, he thought. Her heart-shaped face and carefully styled hair that gave the appearance of having been neglected topped a delicately formed frame that made him want to sweep her into his arms and press his lips to hers each time that he saw her. The fact that she had seemed to be in his path every time he turned around for the past month hadn't made it any easier to make what he had decided was the mature choice to avoid her.

After their first afternoon of tea and flirtation, Jerome and Gwendolyn had become obvious in their contrived opportunities to cross paths 'accidently' nearly every day. Those chance meetings had sometimes resulted in visits in either her or his apartment and the flirtations had become more pronounced until Jerome had made a conscious decision that his attraction, he went so far as to almost call it a 'fixation', had gone too far and he had begun to put as much energy into avoiding her as he had into seeing her.

"Hi!" Gwendolyn said as he began to pass. "I've been missing our talks."

Jerome stopped and turned to her, feeling his stomach tighten as he breathed in her perfume and watching as she turned toward him, then, after a trio of seconds had slipped by, stepped forward.

She's too young, Jerome thought. Jud Carson would say that she had some history but no real mileage. Mostly, he thought, she's too sweet and too nice to put time into me.

Gwendolyn held him steady in her gaze. She was waiting for a response.

"Me, too," he said, wondering again why his breath was so shallow every time that he was around her.

"Well, I, uh, was hoping that we could do something about that," she went on.

"Look I'm sure that you have better things to do with your time," Jerome said with a controlled smile.

Gwendolyn shook her head, tossing her brown hair from side to side and lowering her face again to regard him from beneath her lashes. "You are a most fascinating man," she said softly. She put her left hand behind her as if to press her palm against the column and leaned further back. It was as though she were settling in for a long conversation and inviting him to do so, too, he thought.

The movement had pulled the left side of her waist-length denim jacket back and exposed more of the light cotton blouse below. The loose-weaved white material became nearly transparent when stretched across her breast as she shifted her left foot forward and rested herself, hip-shot, her smile never faltering. Gwendolyn had evidently not felt the need to wear a bra.

"You are very kind," he nearly whispered it. Then, "Have you ever been to the *Saffron*?"

Gwendolyn's smile brightened again and she shook her head.

"How about that, then?" he asked. "We can have dinner and talk all we like."

Gwendolyn nodded. "I'd like that," she said. "I'd like that a lot."

"Saturday?" he asked.

"I'm already looking forward to it," she said.

For an instant they continued to simply stand and look at each other. Jerome fought and managed to resist the temptation to lean forward and brush her cheek with his lips. "Well," he said at last, "I'll see you then."

Gwendolyn nodded again. "Saturday. Seven days. Plenty of time to change my mind about what to wear." She flashed her smile again.

"How does seven o'clock sound?"

"I'll be ready."

"I'll call first."

Gwendolyn rolled her eyes but nodded her head. "Good idea," she laughed. "I'll probably be in the midst of a wardrobe dilemma!"

"I don't think that you could make a bad

choice," Jerome said.

You don't want to know how wrong you are about that, Gwendolyn thought. "But, you know," she said, "you don't have to wait 'til Saturday – give me a call."

"It's going to seem like a month," Jerome said, unwilling to let the conversation, and contact, end.

"Well, it will be a whole new month," Gwendolyn smiled.

"Good point," Jerome said, easing away at last.

I can't believe that I actually asked her out, he thought as he crossed to the elevator and pushed the up button. No, he thought in his best Jud Carson: it's time to tell the truth: you can't believe that she had said 'yes'.

*****

Notebook 24, Entry 17

"Two of Lt. Martinelli's homicide squad, Crayton and Russell, fell in beside me the instant that I stepped onto the sidewalk and guided me to the waiting squad car parked in the alley. Martinelli was in the front passenger seat and I was hustled into the back with a linesman on either side. The tight squeeze made it hard to breathe. The cheap cologne made it worse.

"Which one of you is running the whorehouse?" I asked.

"Martinelli rolled his eyes and sighed. "Cut the comedy, Carson," he said. "We've got to have a chat about your pal Danny Granger."

"Nice guy," I said. "Paid his taxes. Stayed in the

middle of his lane."

"Don't give me that," the lieutenant snapped. "Granger was as easy on the edges as the rest of you peepers."

"He didn't deserve to get capped off in his own house in front of the picture of his sainted mother," I said.

"Martinelli flexed his jaw.

"He saved your ass a time or two," I went on.

"The cop held up a hand to cut me off. He gestured and the driver and two side men got out of the car. They moved to the head of the alley and began to talk amongst themselves.

"Yeah," Martinelli said at last, "Granger did me some solids. He did that for a bunch of us."

"And?"

"And I don't need a bunch of P.I.s running around looking to settle scores."

"I settled back. So that was it. He was putting us on notice that we were to defer to the S.F.P.D. on the case of Daniel Lawrence Granger.

"So you expect us to just trade bubblegum cards and wait while the slow wheel of justice grinds?"

"Martinelli's eyes narrowed and his nostrils flared. It might have made him look funny except for the fact that I knew just how dangerous he could be. This was no dumb flat-foot made rank. He was as tough as they came and knew just how close to the edge of the cliff he could dance.

"Any leads?" I asked.

"Martinelli shook his head. "I was going to ask you

the same thing."

"Nothing. Just found out. What do you know?"

"Small caliber. Close range. Pretty much instantaneous. He never had a chance."

"You know what that means, don't you?" I asked.

"Yeah," Martinelli said. "It means that Granger knew the shooter."

"We were silent for a moment. Then, "I need to know that you and your friends will steer clear of this."

"And feed you what we get."

"Look, Carson, I don't need your help! And if I did…" He stopped, shook his head and seemed to gather his thoughts again. "Yeah, whatever you get," he said.

"I nodded and Martinelli signaled for his men to return. Crayton opened the back door to let me out. "Sorry about Granger," he said softly.

"I nodded again. "You still smell like a whorehouse," I said.

"The crimson silk Chinese dress was split on the side from the floor to her collar. Three tasseled silk cords tied in bows held it together: one on the creamy skin of her right hip, one half-way up her ribcage, and one between her shoulder and neck.

"A mandarin collar with three pearl buttons stood at attention under a delicate chin. The diamond shape of her face seemed to float above the dress, and the green of her eyes matched that of the dragon, accented with gold threads, that wrapped around her waist and curled upward, its open mouth perched on the seat of honor commanding the view from her right breast.

"Her dark auburn hair cascaded down around her shoulders and for a moment I wondered, like most of the other men in the room, what it would be like to be hidden, even lost, in that veil. She seemed so unaware of the effect that she had on a room that there was no doubt that she knew exactly what effect she was having.

"Mr. Carson?" she asked. Her voice was silk rustling on silk. The dress and hairstyle were out of the Far East, but her accent was Back Bay, with touches of a dozen ports of call since. She had been around all right, but always on her own terms.

"I stood and nodded once, then pulled out the chair next to me.

"Have I kept you waiting long?"

"I wondered how she would manage the chair in the suggestion of a dress that she was wearing. It didn't take long to get an answer: Very well.

"No, just long enough," I said. I gestured for the waiter and when he leaned over I whispered 'Two bourbon and branch' in keeping with the former speakeasy's tradition.

"I suppose that you want me to get right to the point," she went on.

"Not especially," I said. "I haven't had my drink yet and I'm enjoying the atmosphere. But if you have somewhere to go…someone to meet…"

"No," she said softly as she glanced around, "it's nothing like that. But, do you think that we are safe here?"

"I took a look around.

"Safe is a relative term. Miss – ?" I raised my eyebrows to emphasize the point that I hadn't been told what to call her yet.

"Merriman," she offered. "Elaine Merriman."

"I smiled and nodded.

" – Merriman." I picked up where I had put the hole in our conversation. "I'd say that we were safe from most things. Excluding earthquakes and tourists. This is San Francisco, after all."

"She glanced around again, this time with more of an apparent concern.

"Look, Miss – " I paused to get a grip on the name that she had given me – "Merriman"

"Her eyes darted back at me like twin vipers.

"You say that like you don't believe me," she said.

"Believe you?"

"That my name is Elaine Merriman."

"I sighed, smiled and shook my head. This was becoming comical. Thankfully, the waiter arrived just in time to break the rhythm of the conversation. After he had placed the drinks, collected, and left, I stirred the brown liquid for a few seconds.

"Quite frankly, I don't care if you call yourself 'Mary Astor'," I said. "I was asked to meet you here to discuss a possible job. That's the extent of my concern." I took a sip of my drink and sat back.

"She seemed to be considering things. Then, "I am sorry, Mr. Carson, I didn't mean to be rude. It's just that I'm frightened. And alone."

"This was a dame that would only be alone when she wanted it that way, I thought. She was as curvy as Lombard Street. And as intriguing. The man who could master the two of them would have a lot to brag about. I had already driven Lombard.

"That's okay," I soothed. "Just relax and tell me all about it."

"There is a letter," she began.

"I nodded.

"A man named Brighton, Jeffrey Brighton, he has it. He stole it from me and I must have it back." She lowered her eyes then used the straw to sip from her drink.

"And you would like me to make sure that that happens?"

"She looked up at me with those green eyes under the veil of her lashes. The straw was still in place in the cupid's bow of her mouth. When she set the glass down there was a suggestion of her crimson lipstick on the straw.

"I spoke to some people who said that you are the type of man I need."

"And you trust those people to know the type of man that you need." I didn't ask – I just laid it out like a low off-suit to see what shook out of the bushes.

"Yes," she said simply. She met my eyes but she wasn't giving anything away.

"Very well," I said, "now let's suppose that I am the

kind of man that you need. And let's suppose that I locate Jeffrey Brighton and ask for your letter back." I took a sip of my bourbon and branch, considered for a moment, then went on. "And let's suppose that he says that he doesn't want to do that." I looked her in the eyes. "What then?"

"She didn't hesitate for more than a breath. "I was told, by some people," she said, "that you were a man who knew what to do. And that you were able to handle anything that came your way." She seemed to sit up a bit more straight and the dragon's mouth seemed to open a bit more as she pulled her shoulders back and thrust his perch further out.

"I tightened my upper lip across my teeth and nodded slowly. So that was it, was it? Someone had put her on to me because the word was that I knew how to shave the edges from the letter of the law and still get the desired results. Or maybe she had been told that I wasn't above dealing from the bottom of the deck if that's what it was going to take to make rent.

"I shook off the implied insult and turned my attention back to the moment. So this letter was that important to her. Well, maybe it was and maybe it wasn't. The question was how important it was going to be to me. I looked at the dragon again and wondered why it was that I seldom got the kinds of things coming my way that I would enjoy.

"From somewhere she had produced five Franklins and placed them on the table between us. Normally I don't like crowds but the seven of us seemed to make for a cozy time.

"Is this enough to get things started?" she asked.

"I looked at the bills and then up at her again. She was a cool one, all right. She had trouble written all over her in a half-dozen languages. I read danger on her like a blind man knows to stand still when his cane stops tapping out the safe step.

"She was the kind of woman that could melt you with her kisses and still have ice in her spine. And the man who held her in his arms, even knowing that she was that kind of a woman, would feel lucky.

"I told myself that I should get up, walk away and never look back. There was enough cash in the roll stashed behind my kitchen stove for me to take a week off and head out of town in case she tried to change my mind. I could suggest a couple of other private eyes who could use the work and weren't discriminating about the source of it. I even knew a couple who deserved to spend time in her company and suffer whatever was going to fall on their heads from the association.

"But the dragon on her breast grinned at me as if it already knew my next words.

"What can you tell me about Jeffrey Brighton?" I asked."

-    *When the Clock Strikes Dead*
  Jud Carson, P.I.

*****

Gwendolyn Dean protested feebly and without conviction. Her thoughts seemed scattered like light in a San Francisco fog. Her tongue felt thick. Too many drinks last night.

His hands were hot and his palm centered on her turgid, bare, and somewhat tender, left nipple as he spooned against her. As she began to swim up to consciousness she felt him begin to press against her; the rhythm was unmistakable and it achieved its aim despite both her desire to go back to sleep and the not-unpleasant ache from the night before. His breath was hot on her neck now and she began to press back against him, equaling his urgency and pressing her left hand down forcefully on his as he rolled her nipple between his forefinger and thumb.

Gwendolyn was surprised by how much she wanted him. He had seemed too shy – and, she would admit it now – too old – to appeal to her. But now…

She pulled his hand away from her breast and tasted his fingers. The sharp tang of old tobacco burned her tongue. I never knew that he smoked, she thought. Too bad, that was something that she had hoped she was done with – men who smoked. Men like – .

The jangling of the phone made her snap her eyes open. Her apartment was bathed in early morning light. Her panties and bra, blouse and skirt were strewn over the floor. She knew that her lover's clothes would have been deposited as haphazardly on the other side of the small room. For an instant confusion ran through her. The phone rang again. Then again. The hand on her breast traveled across her stomach. Then the short, thick fingers were toying with the trimmed, silky hairs that grew above her mound. He gripped her hip and pressed forward, his lips tracing her left shoulder. He nipped at her and she drew a ragged breath, her hips jutting back forcefully and a short moan breaking from her throat was the sound of surrender.

The answering machine in the other room had switched on and given its outgoing message The tone sounded. She always left the monitor on so that she could screen her calls, and, after a brief hesitation, "Gwendolyn, uh, this is – well, I guess you probably know who this is," the caller said. The voice sounded hollow in the empty room. "I thought, if you weren't busy this morning, we could grab some breakfast – or maybe just coffee, if you like." There was a pause. "You have my number. Looking forward to the *Saffron!*"

Gwendolyn Dean's heart sank.

"Hmmm…Gwen, you feel good."

Huey pushed her over onto her stomach, opened her legs by pressing between them with his knees and quickly slid into her with a familiar grunt. Though her body responded to his her mind was far away in a place where she no longer worried about the bills that had to be paid and whether the man she had chosen would come back to her at the end of the day. This was the last time, she knew, that she could have that fantasy. Huey would see to that. She had taken him back and she no longer had any control over how their relationship would go on or where it would end up. She had given that over to the man who could make her orgasm but would never again make her smile.

She struggled with her emotions. A single tear

escaped despite the welling tightness that told her that both she and Huey would be spent once more in no more than a moment's time.

I should have let this story end earlier, she thought. Then she bit her lower lip, hard, and crested the wave with Huey.

Chapter Three

Excerpt, Daily Read File:
Tuesday, 10 September 1989
BBC Monitoring/FBIS

(Budapest, Hungary) In a stunning move today that shook the foundations of both the East and West, the government of Hungary has opened the western borders of the country to refugees from the GDR.

*****

Cold, he thought. And with a mist that constantly threatened, and yet never quite became, rain. It was like spending the evening with a woman who would neither smile nor declare the injury that she felt had been done to her dignity. The misery hung in the air and crowded out what life might have made its cautious way in. He wanted to shift his feet to chase the chill out but he knew that even that movement might be too much. He waited. The shadows had been long when he had made his way down this quiet street from the Ladbroke Grove subway – *tube* – he corrected himself – station. The streetlamp gave but feeble protest to the darkness and he knew that he was well hidden by the nook of an overhang above a side door and the neat and tidy

English alleyway.

He was as uncomfortable here as the West Indians had been in the 1950's. The English racists had beaten and burned their minority brothers and sisters for several days and nights in August and September of 1958. Here, in the very shadow of St. John's church on the top of the hill. Hypocrits. He took a breath and reminded himself that the Notting Hill riots were long in the past and that the Teddy Boys who might be out cruising would not be interested in someone of his ethnicity. And, so long as he did not speak, they would not know that he was a foreigner at all. Those days and nights were long gone. This neighborhood, so close to the famed Kensington Gardens, was now fashionable. It was now – at least *this* portion – reserved for those who had – and had in abundance.

A car made its way slowly from the corner and stopped in front of the house across from his vantage point. The driver glanced around as though conducting a security inspection but it was perfunctory and no more than a checkpoint item. He had made the gesture so many times without actually seeing anything worthy of mention that he no longer even registered what his eyes saw. If it were otherwise he would have seen the man in the alleyway edge further into the shadows.

He turned and said something over his shoulder to the passenger behind him. The rear door opened and a man wearing a dark overcoat emerged. He leaned back into the car, retrieved a package and then closed the door. The driver edged the car away as his passenger straightened and turned toward the steps leading up to the townhouse. He did not see the figure glide out of the shadows behind him and quickly cross the damp street.

Four more steps separated the man from his front door when he heard the voice behind him.

"Sir Thomas?"

Sir Thomas Throckmorton stopped his upward climb but did not turn. He shifted the package to his right hand and placed his left on the black wrought-iron railing that paced the steep steps upward.

"Dancer," he said, using the assigned code name. It was not a question. Sir Thomas had not seen or spoken to his agent in nearly a year but the voice registered as though they had dined together only hours ago.

Dancer shifted his shoulders and thrust his hands into his overcoat. "You must destroy my file and forget that I have existed," he said.

Sir Thomas took a deep breath, sighed, and shook his head slowly. "You know that the game is not played that way." He seemed about to turn around but hesitated then stayed as he was, his back to the man below. "Once you have made your bargain you must see it through."

"But the times have changed, I will be exposed," Dancer protested.

Sir Thomas nodded. "Yes, that is possible," he conceded. "But remember, it will not be to very many. And only I know your true identity. To others you are but a code name."

"That may be, or it may not be, I do not know this," Dancer said. He moved closer to the bottom of the steps. "But I am certain that if you do not do as I ask, when the time comes, there are those who will know me by what I have told you. And that will be the end of me."

Sir Thomas shifted his weight to the left. "That may be," he said, "but that is the bargain you made for the reward you wanted. And we have paid you just as you demanded. There can be no denying that, Dancer, we have paid you, and paid you well."

"Not enough for my life," Dancer hissed. "I will be arrested. I may be killed."

"You knew that these were the risks that we take," Sir Thomas argued. "You came to us, remember, we did not seek you out and tempt you."

For a moment neither man spoke. Then, "You will not release me?" Dancer asked.

"There is too much that you can still do for us," Sir Thomas said. "And you will be paid, as always."

"You are the only one who knows me?" Dancer went on. There was a change in the tone of his voice, a resignation, as though he were accepting the inevitable.

Sir Thomas nodded. "You can rest assured that that is the truth," he said reassuringly, as though he were comforting one of his grandchildren who had awakened from a bad dream.

Dancer covered the intervening distance in one stride, his right hand coming clear of his overcoat and the stiletto flashing dully in the heavy air before it jabbed forward. The tip sliced through the older man's overcoat between the shoulder blades, skidded off a rib and drove into his heart then withdrew. The package in the old man's right hand dropped to the steps and Dancer heard glass breaking. Then Sir Thomas has falling backward and Dancer moved out of his way, letting the old man stumble and fall onto the sidewalk below.

Dancer moved back down and knelt beside Sir Thomas. The old man struggled to breathe and his eyes did not seem to be able to register what they saw. Much like his driver, he looked for danger, but did not see it. The stiletto struck again and the light that had first shown some seventy-plus years earlier in Sir Thomas Throckmorton's eyes dimmed and went out. The cold warrior would soon be as cold as the London night in which he lay. Dancer slipped the stiletto blade between the dead man's suit jacket and the vest beneath it, pressed down on his overcoat above and wiped the weapon clean.

Dancer pulled Sir Thomas's wallet from his coat and stood, turning away from the body and slipping the knife and stolen wallet into his pockets.

He did not hurry away. He walked slowly, his head down against the chill night and feeble lights. The wallet was emptied of cash and credit cards and left wedged in the seat of a bus. In an alley he used a cigarette lighter to melt the credit cards; they were dropped into a storm drain. The stiletto, gloves and coat were discarded in different trash bins between Sir Thomas Throckmorton's town home and Heathrow International Airport.

It would be some time before MI-6 began considering that one of the old man's own operatives had murdered him, if they reached that conclusion at all. Besides, with all of the excitement that was going on in the Eastern Bloc, they had more than enough to keep them busy. He managed to sleep on the flight back to the continent.

*****

The look on her face told him that Gwendolyn had not expected to see him when the elevator door opened. Jerome was as surprised by her sudden appearance, but, considering the fact that he had been leaving unanswered phone messages for three days and had managed to miss her comings and goings as well, he had decided to make a concerted effort to speak to her face-to-face. The trip up one floor had paid off. He felt the knot in his stomach tighten.

For an instant they stared at one another without moving. The elevator doors began to close and Jerome put a hand out, breaking the electronic beam and they slid back into their pockets. "Hi," he said simply.

Gwendolyn nodded and looked down. There was no glance back up through her lashes. There was no quick smile.

"Look, uhmm," he began, stepping into the hallway. "I, uh, called several times." He let his words settle into the distance between them. When she held her silence he went on. "Should I just not do that anymore?"

The doors tried to close again and Gwendolyn stepped forward, keeping them open and turning toward him, half in and half out of the enclosure.

"Well, I've been thinking," she said softly. Gone was the excitement that had carried through in even her quietest voice before. Now the subtle tones were a barrier rather than an invitation. "I've made some pretty bad choices lately. I don't want to make another one."

"And that 'one' would be me." Jerome said. He stepped back from her. He saw her lips move but didn't hear what she had said. The blood pounding in his ears was too loud. Whatever it was that she had said to him, it had been final. The doors to the elevator closed and he was alone in the hallway. He watched his finger move out and push the button marked 'Down'.

*****

Excerpt, Daily Read File:
Tuesday, 9 October 1989
BBC Monitoring/FBIS

(Berlin, FRG) More than 70,000 East Germans protested government policies in the city of Leipzig as part of the "Monday Demonstrations". Protesters gathered despite wide-spread rumors that authorities have ordered a "shoot and kill" policy. This follows the visit of Soviet leader Gorbachev who has publicly urged a shift toward reform in the satellite nation.

*****

"Our man in the Stasi is becoming more and more frightened," Florian Schumann said. Paula Layman set aside the file that she had been reading and gave him her undivided attention. She watched as the old man crossed over to the window of her office. He stood with his back to her, his large, gentle hands clasped behind him. She had enjoyed his caress for nearly a year now. Rarely did she think about how those hands had been put to use in his youth. That had been war.

It had been five months since she had delivered the first contact information. Early on the Stasi man had been unwilling to give away much information and had demanded a great deal in return. Now, with the taste of reform on the tongue of every citizen in the Soviet Bloc, he was becoming more desperate.

No longer was he insisting on a retirement home in Florida with a generous retirement. A passport to a neutral country without extradition and a modest sum of money had been the last price. In a week he might settle for a head-start on his prosecutors.

"He is convinced now that the system is going to fall," Florian went on at last. He turned and looked at her. "That would mean that the Stasi files will be in the hands of the West."

"And in the hands of the East German people," Paula added.

Florian nodded. "This is what he fears most."

"That'll make for a hot time in the old town," Paula said.

Florian smiled, remembering the song. "'A Hot Time in the Old Town Tonight' you know this song?"

Paula nodded and returned the smile. She hummed a bit of the tune.

"And I know another one that you may remember, *mein Herr*." She tapped her fingers on the desk top for a moment as she sought and recalled the first line, then, "We march by the banks of Ruhr and Rhine. And we smash the Hitler Youth in twain." Paula stopped and looked at the elderly man who at once seemed surprised, pleased and shocked.

"Our song is freedom, love and life, We're the Pirates of the Edelweiss," he said, finishing the stanza from a song of his youth.

"But you are so young to know this!" Florian said. "You still surprise me."

"And you surprise me!" Paula replied. "There aren't many of the Germans who fought the Nazis from inside the country still working."

Schumann sighed and glanced around the room. "There aren't so many who survived," he said.

The Pirates, as they had called themselves, were Germans in their teens and early twenties who had rebelled against Hitler and his henchman beginning in the mid 30's. Most had contented themselves with painting slogans and distributing leaflets.

Others, like Schumann, had hidden and transported Jews and other enemies of the state before the war, and downed Allied flyers and POWs after the outbreak of hostilities. A few had raided Nazi military posts for weapons and explosives.

There were surviving reports that 150 German Wehrmacht army soldiers had died for their *fuhrer* when their transport train was derailed over the Loisach River outside of Wolfratshausen by the man who stood before her. He was then 17 years old.

"You were very brave," she said.

"We were very young," he countered. "And, that was so many years ago." He took a deep breath and shrugged his shoulders. "The work must still go on."

"Same fight, different enemy?" she asked.

"Much the same enemy," he answered. "And

just as with the Nazis, there will be much information that comes from the Stasi when the fall comes."

Paula noted that this was the first time that he had said "when" in regard to what some others had considered the imminent and still others thought of as a vague but eventual collapse of the Soviet house of cards. Those of Florian's generation had tended to see the struggle as cyclic and on-going. They remembered the Prague Spring when Dubček had tried to break the Soviet stranglehold on Czechoslovakia only to see the tanks roll in and crush the eight-month-old peaceful reform movement. The Warsaw Pact had stormed into the country and settled the issue in typically brutal fashion.

More recently, the Chinese communists had crushed protesting dissidents in the Tiananmen Square Massacre of June fourth. Thousands had been killed by their own government for daring to suggest even minor reform. Leaders of the movement were still being tracked down at home and abroad.

Few of the old guard thought that the Soviet core would allow the protests in their front yard to continue unchecked while The Chi-Com crushed the anti-revolutionists in their back yard. It would be just a matter of time, they said, until the hard liners seized control from Gorbachev and stabilized the Soviet satellites again. There would be purges and statements and the world would return to its normal, high-tension state.

Now, even Florian was considering that the fall of the Iron Curtain was a real and immediate possibility.

"What is he offering now?" Paula asked.

"He says that he has the names of some

double-agents. We can have them for certain –
assurances."

"Like a "Get out of Jail Free" card?"

The old man nodded. He turned to look out of
the window again. "I don't know," he mused. "It may
be time to pull him out. But, if it is too soon, we will
lose a great deal of information about the plans of the
East German response."

There was a single, light tap on the door and a
young woman entered with the blue daily read file.
She walked directly to Paula who took the file and
signed Florian's initials to the receipt.

"But this Stasi man," Florian began again. "He
says that – "

"Herr Schumann," Paula said, cutting him off,
"Fraulein Kurtz has brought you the read file."

Florian turned, with a slightly confused look on
his face. It seemed to take him a bit to realize that he
was no longer alone with his private confidant. "Ah,"
he said at last. "Danke, Fraulein Kurtz." He walked
over to the desk. Paula stood and stepped toward
him, handing the file over and meeting his questioning
eye.

Florian nodded once to her and then turned to
the young woman.

"Will there be anything else, sir?" she asked.
Her German was accented from Bavaria.

Florian shook his head. "No, thank you." He
flipped the folder open and pretended to be reading.
Even Kurtz knew that the old man would see little but
a blur without his glasses but she did not react.
Instead she nodded once to Paula, turned and left the
room, closing the door quietly behind her.

"How bad was that?" Florian asked without

looking up.

Paula shrugged. "That depends."

"On?"

"On whose side she's on."

"I am too old for this game," Florian sighed.

"No," Paula protested. "But you are tired. Besides, don't worry about her – Kurtz is cleared for most of what goes on around here. We can do a debrief with her later today. She might not have even heard you."

"You did. You stopped this old, deaf fool from going on."

"Yes, but I still listen to you. Most young women don't." Paula smiled. "You need to relax. This thing is going to keep picking up speed until it makes it to the station or jumps the track."

Florian nodded. "Yes," he agreed. "A nice weekend would help. You will come to the country with me this weekend?"

"I'd love to," she answered. "But will we be alone?"

"Except for the staff."

"Then I accept."

*****

Excerpt, Daily Read File:
Wednesday, 18 October 1989
BBC Monitoring/FBIS

(Berlin, FRG) In a move that has been anticipated, but that has still managed to send shock waves across both sides of the Iron Curtain, East Germany's

Communist leader, Erich Honecker has stepped down as that country's chief of state, citing serious health issues.

*****

Claire Hornsby-Colfield smiled graciously at the doorman and then moved past him in practiced elegance and into the lobby of the Hotel Prince de Galles at 33 Place de Gaules. As she passed beneath the crystal chandelier, the desk manager emerged from the door beside the reception area and hurried across the white marble floor. They stopped the requisite three paces from one another and the middle-aged hotelier bowed briefly. "It is so good to see you again, Madame. You do us a great honor by being our guest once again."

Claire smiled genuinely and offered her hand which was dutifully and chastely kissed. "I wouldn't want to stay anywhere else when I am in your city, Henri." She turned her head slightly as Dare entered the lobby and made his way quickly to her side.

"We would be devastated if we were to lose your patronage," Henri responded. He gestured and the bell captain appeared at his side, two assistants trailing him. He pointed and spoke in hushed tones briefly and the two younger men busied themselves retrieving the trunks and cases that had been brought into the lobby by the outside valet staff.

"Madame," Henri began hesitantly, "I know that you requested room 303 once more, but I would be remiss if I did not mention that, while it is an excellent accommodation, it is a standard arrangement. Since your reservation was made we have had a deluxe room become available…" he let the invitation linger.

Claire shook her head, but only slightly. "Henri, every room here is deluxe. But I love the way that the blue in number 303 brings out the color in my husband's eyes." She glanced at Dare who rolled his eyes. She flashed a smile at him and winked. Then, turning back to the manager, "When I am in Paris, the Hotel Prince de Galles, room 303, is my only address. From room 303 I can look out and see the Eiffel Tower and know that all is right with the world."

"And may it always be so," Henri said. He turned and noted that the luggage was already on its way up in the service elevator while the guest elevator was open and waiting. The Colfields, accompanied by the dapper manager, stepped across the lobby and into the brass and polished oak lift followed by the bell captain who extended his hand and took the room key from the manager.

The couple did not speak until they had reached the room, the bags had been situated and the bell crew tipped and dismissed.

"He's got a point, you know," Dare said from the bathroom where he was undoing his tie. He hung it on the hook on the back of the door and pulled his shirt tails out.

Claire was busy kicking off her high heels and digging her feet into the thick carpet.

"Leave your heels on," Dare called.

Claire sighed but put the crème colored shoes back on her tired feet. She unhooked and unzipped her skirt, let it fall around her feet and stepped free of it. She caught a glimpse of herself in the mirror above the writing desk and took a moment to assess what she saw. There was no denying that she was getting older, but the life of a millionaire was slowing and inhibiting the process. If she had gained weight in the last five years it was measured in ounces. She still had a dancer's body and more than a little of a dancer's attitude. The years kicking her legs in Las Vegas shows had produced a discipline that continued long after her next meal depended on how she looked. She continued to watch herself as her lithe fingers undid the small pearl-like buttons of her blouse.

She dropped the silk material to the floor and reached around to undo the bone-colored brassiere. After she had lowered the shoulder straps and tossed it on top of the blouse, itself only a half-shade lighter in tone, she removed the combs from her hair and shook the honey-blonde tresses until they fell in waves just past her shoulders.

"I love this place," she answered her husband, though it was just as much to herself. She pushed her slip down and let it fall. Clad only in her panties she looked at herself in the mirror again. And she waited.

Dare emerged from the bathroom and stepped up behind her, slipping his hands around her from behind. He massaged her stomach gently. "Long flight," he said.

"Uh-huh," she answered, letting her head fall back against his chest.

He moved his hands up onto her ribcage and stroked her while breathing her in. "Tired – but we can't sleep yet – or we'll be up at two in the morning."

Claire let her body sag against him and mewed softly.

"We're going to have to find something to do," Dare went on, letting his hands slide up to cup her breasts. "Any ideas?"

"Uh-huh," Claire said, turning in his arms and stretching up to kiss him gently. When Dare lifted her from her feet she stroked her hands through his hair and whispered, "I love the way the color in this room makes your eyes look."

"And I love you," Dare said. He turned, covered the two paces to the bed and laid her down on the cool sheets. When had he managed to turn the bed down? she asked herself. No doubt while she was wondering about her looks and concentrating on the image in the mirror. What must he think of her? Then Dare's mouth found hers and she forgot about her efforts to chastise herself.

Chapter Four

Fraulein Kurtz rushed into and through her apartment, spilling her shopping bags and ramming a hip into the counter as she careened to a halt at the counter of her small kitchen. She dropped her keys, which slid into the sink as she reached for the still ringing phone on the wall beneath the cupboard. Unclipping her right earring with her left hand she brought the phone up to her head too quickly and tapped her ear smartly with the receiver.

"Hallo?" she managed at last.

"Andelisa?"

"Yes!" She forgot her discomfort at the sound of his voice. "I was so hoping that it was you! I just rushed in and spilled everything to get to the phone before you could hang up! What?" He had been speaking during her report and she suddenly realized that she had not been listening to a word in her hurried explanation of why she had kept him waiting.

"Andelisa, I cannot come to see you this weekend," he repeated.

"This is two weeks in a row!" She hoped that he could hear her pout over the telephone line. "If you do not come to see me I will never speak to you again!" She knew that he was fully aware that it was an empty threat but she did not care.

"I know, Little One," he soothed. She sighed and pulled the kitchen chair back from the small dinette table and plopped down on it. "But it can't be helped."

"And I went to that funny little shop that you like so much and bought something that I knew you would like to see me wear!" She kicked off her high heels and scrunched her toes.

"Tell me about it," he urged.

"No," she said. "It is for you to see – not to hear about."

"Well, then," he said, his voice as gentle as though he were speaking to a troubled child, "perhaps you could show me tonight."

"Tonight?" She brightened again.

"Within the hour," he said. "I have business nearby and I will be able to see you before."

"See me after," she countered. "We will have more time."

"I wish that I could, but I must be elsewhere after. But, if you would rather that I not come to see you at all…"

"No!" she near-shouted, instantly regretting it. "I will have all ready for you," she said.

"By seven tonight, then," he said.

"Until then," she agreed.

Within the hour Fraulein Kurtz had showered, changed into the newly purchased black lace bra and panty set, donned the red silk robe that her lover had bought for her months earlier, and prepared a salad. The wine that currently chilled in the refrigerator was not his favorite, but she had intended to buy that on Friday before he arrived. Well, he would have to make do, she thought. She hoped that he would not be too disappointed in the wine. Or the dinner. Or her.

She perched on the couch in the small living room, sighed, and checked the time again. He might be as much as another thirty minutes. Why was she so concerned that nothing she had or did or was could be good enough for him, she wondered. She was young and smart, and had a good job working for an important man. She was beautiful by most men's standards and, if she was well aware of that fact she did not flaunt it. Too much. Her figure was full and her skin was flawless. Her pale blue eyes were large and well-spaced. Her lips were full and suggested delights. Though she dressed appropriately at work, her figure could not be secreted. Men longed for her. Powerful men. And, she suspected, so did some of the women.

None of that mattered to her. She could think of only one lover. And, despite her charms and ample physical gifts, he left her speechless, breathless, and yearning for the smallest praise from his lips.

The door clicked. He had let himself in with the key she had given him. She felt her heart race and her body begin to tingle. An instant later she was in his arms, her arms about his neck, his mouth working with and against hers, and his hands cupping her ass through the robe.

When he eased back from her she undid the robe and let it fall open. He pushed the silk aside and admired her purchase.

"Have you eaten?" she asked.

"I don't have time to do everything," he said with a thin, lascivious smile.

"A salad – or – me?" she teased. "Which would you rather have?"

"What kind of salad?"

"Beast!" she laughed. Turning toward the short hallway she let the robe fall from her shoulders and puddle on the carpet as she made her way to the bedroom.

He took her from behind as she was crawling across the comforter, catching her about the waist with a powerful hand and stripping the black lace to her knees. She could feel the fabric of his trousers against her thighs; he had not undressed, merely tugged down his zipper and freed himself. She had barely enough time to catch her breath before he had driven into her and drawn the first deep, guttural moan from deep within her. She snatched a pillow from its place at the headboard, lowered her face into its downy softness and raised her hips higher, thrusting back as forcefully as he drove forward. Within a moment he had given her release and let her slip forward, prone and face down on the bed.

With his initial onslaught satisfied they rested briefly. Then she rose, turned down the bed and slipped out of her bra, knowing that he enjoyed both seeing and feeling her bare flesh. She padded down the hall and into the kitchen, retrieved and opened the wine and set a tray with glasses before returning. He had finished undressing and was waiting tucked in her bed as though it were his nightly place. She conceded to herself that she wished it would be that way. And soon.

"How was your day?" she asked. She set the tray on the bureau and carefully poured into the glasses. She had decided not to mention the wine's inferior grade. She tended to apologize too much, she thought. And he had just demonstrated how much he longed for her. He hadn't even been able to wait until he had undressed! Perhaps she should be more assertive, she thought.

* * *

"Nothing special," he answered, taking the glass that she offered. They each sipped and, if he did not approve of the wine, at least he did not say so.

"And yours?"

She sat her glass on the nightstand and leaned over him so that he could touch her breasts with his free hand. She smiled and tossed her blonde hair, stretched her back and sighed contentedly. He was arousing her again. She glanced down and acknowledged that he was becoming so again, too. "I thought that my poor boss might have a heart-attack today," she said lazily.

"How so?" his voice was sharper than she had expected. But his hand continued to stroke her, and his forefinger and thumb were having the desired effect on her nipples.

"I heard him talking about – something – I guess that I wasn't supposed to."

"And what was that?"

"Oh, you know, I'm not supposed to talk about anything that happens at work," she said, in a feeble attempt to be interesting to her lover without breaking the rules of her employment.

He tweaked her nipple and made her sigh again. "What was it?" he pressed.

Andelisa shook her head again. "Not supposed to tell," she teased.

She closed her eyes as he sat up, leaned forward and captured her turgid flesh between his teeth. "Come on, tell me," he urged. His tongue was sending ripples of pleasure through her.

"Something about – " she gasped as he reached between her legs and touched her center.

"Yes?"

She mumbled but his attentions and her thick Bavarian accent had made her speech undecipherable.

"What was that?"

"Their Stasi man telling them something. They were very excited about it," she said. "Now, no more questions for now!" She rose, pulled back the covers and straddled him. Taking his length and leaning down to press her lips to his she managed to take the glass from his hand and set it on the nightstand beside her own before beginning to rise and fall more forcefully on him. She did not see him reach down beside the bed and retrieve the bra that she had bought to wear for him.

Chapter Five

Even the Schumann estate staff, which never seemed to be surprised by anything, was visibly put off by the arrival of Frau Schumann. The grande dame's car had pulled up to the front door and she had been escorted inside by Florian's nephew, Berrin, nearly before any of the household had become aware of her presence.

Florian and Paula, already at dinner, had suffered the awkward moment with diplomacy and she had nodded to Florian, and even given Paula a small nod when her husband of nearly forty years had told her that they would be working over the weekend. With her dignity intact, she had retired to dine alone in her rooms upstairs.

When she had gone Florian turned his attention to his nephew.

"I tried to call," Berrin offered, "but she insisted that we come here straightaway and you know how demanding your wife can be, Uncle."

Florian nodded. "I had thought that she would be staying in the city this weekend," he mused. "How did you come to be the one to drive her?"

It was no secret that Frau Schumann did not drive. And, if at all possible, she would not have taken a taxi. That meant that she either travelled by rail, plane, ship, or chauffeur. And, on occasion, by nephew.

The chauffeur was here at the estate.

"I wanted to show Aunt Walburga a rare book

that I had found in Bavaria and so I stopped by." He shrugged. "She decided that it was more important that she come here to spend the weekend."

Paula stood and started for the doorway. "If you will excuse me, gentlemen, I really should be going."

Florian waived his hand, and stood. "No, Paula – " he glanced at Berrin who pretended not to notice. "Please, everything is arranged – please stay the night and we can begin the work the first thing in the morning."

Paula shook her head once and left the room. Florian caught her a few steps further, taking her elbow gently. "Please, *Liebshen*," Florian pleaded, "there is no reason to leave."

"Really?" she asked, snatching her arm away and taking a half-step back from him. "Your wife shows up and you don't think that it might be bad form for your lover to stay under the same roof with her? What were you thinking?"

"I did not know that she was coming!" he whispered, then, reacting to the sound of approaching footsteps, he, too, stepped back. Cook emerged from the dining room and was bearing a tray for Frau Schumann. They waited until he had passed up the stairs and turned down the hall to the suite of rooms reserved for her.

Paula eyed Florian cautiously. "Are you sure you didn't know?" she asked. "An old spy like you doesn't know what his own wife is planning?"

"I swear it," Florian said simply. There was no effort to persuade. It was a simple statement and it achieved its goal.

Paula nodded once. "All right," she said. "I

believe you. But I should go."

Florian sighed heavily. "Please, stay," he whispered. "The work must be done, after all."

Paula tapped her foot in the distracted way that he had come to recognize as her sign of irritation. She crossed her arms tightly and was about to speak when the downstairs maid crossed the room toward the servant's hallway.

Florian saw his opening and positioned himself to exploit it. "She will not leave her rooms tonight. She will never know that you have."

"No damned way, Florian Schumann!" Paula hissed. "I am not going to go to your bed while your wife is down the hall!"

"She will be in the other side of the house," he insisted.

"Don't you dare ask me that again," Paula said, glowering. "I am not on the dessert tray tonight!"

Florian raised his hands, palms toward her in a gesture of surrender. "I will not ask again, Paula, but, please, please stay the weekend. It will be more obvious if you leave now."

Paula considered for a moment; then she nodded. He was right. To leave now would be as much as a confession to Florian's wife. Not that the grand dame did not know what had been planned – what had been going on, even, for all these months. But it would be an insult that she could not ignore. Paula would have to be dismissed. There would be a scandal, although one at the highest levels of society and government, and Paula would be the one to suffer the most. She had been through this act of the play before and she had no intention of reprising her role.

She shook her head and glanced about the room in order to avoid meeting Florian's eyes. Marcus, the butler, was standing in the doorway of the study, holding a telephone.

"There is a call for Herr Schumann," he said in his careful monotone. There was no sign that he had witnessed the altercation. There was also no doubt in Paula's mind that he had heard every word that had passed between them.

"You will stay?" Florian asked, his eyes never straying from Paula.

She nodded. "But just plan on sleeping alone tonight," she said. "I'm going to my room now and I won't be leaving it until in the morning." She tried but failed to appear calm and relaxed as she made her way up the stairs.

*****

The polizei did not knock or otherwise announce themselves. One moment Paula was asleep, happily not dreaming, and the next she was awake, her arms held by officers on either side of the bed and the comforting darkness was driven away by the blast of every light in the room being turned on. When her mind registered what was happening she had already been screaming for several seconds. With an efficiency that gave rise to stereotypes the German police flipped her onto her back and had the handcuffs on her wrists before she had stopped.

Since she was already nude they did not frisk her but a female officer quickly found a pair of panties, some walking shorts, a bra and blouse for her to dress in. She helped Paula sit up, her buttocks resting on her heels as she balanced in the center of the bed. The woman draped the top sheet around her, affording her a modicum of recovered dignity as her heart pounded in her chest.

"If we remove the handcuffs, you will dress, yes?" the woman asked her.

Paula nodded once and stifled another scream. "What is this about?" she managed to whisper.

The female officer, perhaps five years younger than Paula herself, flicked her eyes toward the far side of the room where two other officers were methodically going through the drawers of the bureau. One reached in with a gloved hand and carefully lifted out the automatic pistol nestled among Paula's folded blouses and sweaters. As she watched, the officer sniffed the barrel of the weapon and nodded to his partner who held out an open evidence bag.

A tall, older officer approached. Clearly, Paula thought, this is the one in charge of the hootenanny. The female officer held the sheet closer around Paula.

"Fraulein Layman," the man said. "We will be detaining you."

"Do I get to know why?" Paula asked.

"Your employer has been murdered. We have reason to believe that your gun," he nodded to the bureau where the officer who had found the weapon was making out a document that could establish the chain of evidence, "was used. That is your gun, is it not?"

She wanted to protest that she was innocent. That the gun wasn't hers, really. Florian had given it to her but it wasn't something that she had wanted. She wanted to scream that she hadn't screwed up in a long, long time and that she had vowed that she never would again. She wanted to tell this man that when she had been a screw-up it had been mostly drinking and screwing and never shooting. Even now she could feel her nipples stiffen and her areola crinkle, as if she were preparing to bargain her way out of her situation, but she knew that it was only an instinctive fear reaction.

She took a deep breath and let it out slowly. "I would like," she said carefully, "to speak to someone from the American embassy, please."

Within twenty minutes she was dressed and bundled into her overcoat. The female officer held her wrists, now handcuffed behind her, as Paula made her way down the broad staircase. One of the male officers moved slowly in front of her. While they waited in the foyer, Marcus, who had been trusted by Florian to run the household for longer than Paula had been alive, stepped forward and draped a scarf around her neck. When the polizei officer at the door seemed about to interfere the retainer had glowered coldly. "This is a civilized home," he said. "Fraulein Paula is a guest. We do what is right." The officer had retreated.

"I will have your favorite dinner waiting when you return," Marcus said gently. He reached into the pocket of his robe and withdrew a handkerchief. He dabbed her eyes gently, as though she were a child and then he tucked the cloth into the pocket of her overcoat.

Then the door opened and the flashing lights of the police car flooded the foyer. A moment later Paula was securely tucked into the back seat and the car was speeding away.

*****

In the days since their arrival in Paris, Claire Hornsby-Colfield had managed to pry her attorney-business-manager-husband away from work on only two of the five mornings. Afternoons were dedicated to the business meetings that consumed his energy and left little for her to enjoy even in what was considered by many to be the most romantic city in Europe. At least most of the people that Claire had grown up with would have voted Paris as the most romantic.

Many Americans would consider it the most rude and many Europeans would call it the most over-rated. Claire had always found it to be fascinating and the object of many of her desires. Having an open mind to others helped her to overcome many of the prejudices that others held against Paris and the Parisians. Having a husband who was fluent in the native language and could, for the most part, mimic the local accent helped to overcome most of the indignities that other guests of the city endured. Having a great deal of money seemed to take care of whatever else might interfere with her pleasure.

On the morning after their arrival she left Dare to sleep in and taxied the two miles between the Hotel Prince de Galles and the Louvre, arriving just as it was opening at nine. She took her time, as always, wandered galleries and studied one piece after another before deciding to spend time with Ghirlandaio's duel portrait of a disfigured old man and an angelic young boy. She had seen it before on an earlier visit and it had made her think instantly of her deceased first husband. So much so, in fact, that she had hurried by it. Now she studied it and came to terms with the work.

Like the Florentine patrician, Edmund had been patient and kind to her, knowing that, although he was the source of her comfort, the most that she would ever be able to give to him would be the joy he had being in her company. Like the boy in the painting, she had not been able to understand Edmund's generosity to her at the time. The rest of the morning she spent in the same hall, considering other works, but, each time, returning to the Ghirlandaio. This, she acknowledged, would be her French lesson learned on this trip.

The afternoon was spent on the Champs Elysees, looking at everything and buying nothing. From here it was only a few minutes' walk to the hotel where she bathed and met Dare for dinner in the hotel's restaurant before they moved to the Regency Bar for nightcaps. Despite the travel and stress of his meetings Dare was, as ever, gallant and attentive. He was, however, asleep within minutes of retiring to their rooms.

He had taken Friday to spend with her. A trip to the Eiffel Tower, which had become *de rigueur*, included lunch at the *Jules Verne*. After an afternoon in the Tuileries gardens, they dined at an open-air café and walked the Alexandre III Bridge over the Seine, joining the Champs Elysees and Les Invalides. Having adjusted to the time-zone, work, and to Paris itself, Dare was more of the ardent suitor that she remembered from their earliest courtship.

Saturday she contented herself with trips to the *beaux quartiers* and hours in the Petit Palais museum. Sunday had been quiet for both of them. The business meetings were complete, he assured her and the rest of the trip would be devoted to them.

Everything changed on Sunday evening when Dare had received the phone call. Its importance was beyond doubt. One moment he had been laughing and adjusting his tie while waiting for her to finish putting in the earrings he had just given to her. Ten minutes later he was explaining that he would have to catch the next plane to Berlin. An old friend was in need and he could not refuse. She should stay and enjoy herself, he said, distractedly looking about the room. Oh, yes, he would have to have his suitcase sent up, and he would have to pack a few things. Could she remember where he had put his wallet? He had had it just a moment ago.

Claire had finally taken her husband's hands and forced him to sit with her on the bed. They would go together, she said. He should change into travel clothes and she would see to everything. He had seemed to have trouble focusing on her at first, but, at last, he had nodded. He supposed so. Claire waited until he had gone into the bathroom and quietly closed the door before picking up the phone and asking for Henri.

As she waited Claire turned to the windows. She could see the lights of the Eifel Tower as they climbed the structure to the top.

"*Oui*, Madam, this is Henri," the manager said.

Claire turned her eyes away from the window. "Henri, something has gone wrong," she said.

Monsieur and Madam would reach their destination before dawn the hotelier assured her a few minutes later. Ten minutes later she opened the door to the discrete tapping, admitting the bell captain and two of his subordinates. He bowed slightly and handed her an envelope containing their passports then began directing the packing of their belongings. When Dare emerged from the bathroom the two of them made their way to the elevators and began on their journey to the occupied city of Berlin.

Chapter Six

Excerpt, Daily Read File:
Monday, 23 October 1989
BBC Monitoring/FBIS

The Kremlin establishment has had no immediate response to the announcement made today by Hungary's President Mátyás Szűrös that the Hungarian People's Republic has been dissolved and replaced by the Hungarian Republic. Residents of Budapest are reportedly bracing for an expected Soviet assault to end such democratic reforms in the satellite nations.

*****

Jerome Carstead cocked his head toward the ringing phone in the other room. Setting the coffee pot back in its place he picked up the full cup beside it and made his way out of the kitchen, across the small dining room and into the living room with its bay windows overlooking San Francisco's Post Street. The album jacket for *The Singing City* was propped in the stereo's cabinet. He picked up the record player arm and used the needle brush on the diamond tip then placed it carefully on the black platter in the empty space after *In my Liverpool Home*. The

Spinners' version of Ewan McColl's *Dirty Old Town* began. Carson's phone continued to ring and he took a deep breath before answering.

"Hello." There was no invitation to conversation. The perfunctory greeting was meant to inform the caller of one thing: he was listening. In the one word he had established himself; gone from his voice was the easy-going roundness. He had pulled the detective's voice off the shelf and donned it as he would the old tan trench-coat hanging in the closet. He had learned the hard way that when Jud Carson's number was called, it was Jud Carson who had to answer.

"Jud? This is Dare."

Jerome felt his face flush. The detective-persona nearly slipped as the flood of emotion swept through him. Colfield was one of the few that he considered a friend. Over the past few years their communications had been more and more infrequent, but, when the connection was made it was still strong. They were bonded by shared experience, and, though neither would voice it, perceived mutual debt.

"Mouth-piece," Jerome managed. "Long time, no hear – still abusing the orphans?" He avoided the traditional 'widows and orphans' out of deference to Claire, who's widowing had brought the three of them together in the first place.

"Of course," Dare answered. Jerome took a breath. The lawyer had not come back with an equally friendly insult. Something was wrong.

"Is Claire all right?" he asked.

"Yeah, sure, she's fine," Dare responded, then, quickly, "I am, too."

Jerome let himself feel the relief. "Well, thanks

for that," he chided, "but what makes you think that I was especially interested in you? Claire, on the other hand…"

"You know how she feels about you," the lawyer said.

"Yeah. Too bad." Jerome sighed. "So to what do I owe this call?"

"I need your help," Dare said quietly.

Jerome felt his stomach tighten.

"Like before?"

"Pretty much."

"I thought you said that Claire – "

"It's not Claire – or me. There's someone else – someone you don't know."

Jerome held his silence.

Colfield seemed to sense the unasked question after a few silent seconds. "No, not like that, either," he said. "But she – "

"'She'?"

"Yeah, 'She'," Colfield said. "She and I do have a, well, a 'history'."

"Is that where this call is coming from?" Jerome asked.

"No, this is a totally present-day problem."

"What kind of problem is that?" Jerome picked up his pen and began to doodle on the blotter.

"The kind that I always call you for," Colfield said. "It's murder."

For a moment the two men let the silence settle between them. Then Colfield cleared his throat and went on, "Can you come take a look at the situation? I'm holding a flight booking for Saturday – I know it's short notice."

"It always is," Jerome said. Then, "Sure," he

said, "I've got nothing going on Saturday night; it'll give me something to do."

*****

Notebook 24, Entry 18

"I had spotted the tail as I slipped Elaine Merriman's phone number – I recognized it as one of the city's finer hotels – into my pocket and before I could even consider how I was going to track Jeffrey Brighton down in a city the size of San Francisco.

"He was too big to be doing that kind of work and the tweed jacket that he wore was expensive and well-tailored but you wouldn't know it by the way that he had stretched it over his broad back and chest. It made him almost like a parody. The obvious bulge of a rod under his left arm decreased my sense of levity. He was doing his best to look inconspicuous at the news and tobacco stand across from the *Bourbon and Branch* but he might as well have been waiving a flag for all the good it did.

"It didn't take a team from Stanford to figure out the play. He had followed her to the speak and seen her meet with me. Now he would tag one of us and I had a feeling that he already knew something about Elaine Merriman that I had not – where she was hanging her glad rags when it was time to call it a full day of intrigue. That meant that he would be more likely to try to cut sign on me instead. I walked to the corner and turned toward the bay. It would be easier for him to keep track of me if I were going down the hill. At least it would be until I decided just how I wanted to play him.

"My hunch turned out and I could hear him crossing the damp street behind me. A minute later I started making a series of zig-zags along the narrowing streets: first a turn to the west, then one to the north. They weren't obvious moves to shake a tail, in fact, my pace hadn't picked up at all. But I knew where I was going and what I was going to do when I got there. My traveling companion was, figuratively, in the dark.

"Then the lights did go out for him when I turned into an alley, slipped down a half-flight of stairs and pushed through the unlocked delivery door of my favorite laundry. I leaned against the door and listened for him to enter the alley. When he did I could sense his frustration. There was nowhere to turn out of the alley for quite a ways and yet he couldn't see me up ahead. It took only a few seconds for him to realize and accept that he had managed to lose me. All right. Now what? Do what thugs always do: go back to the one with the brain and let them figure it out. His shoe leather scuffed and he turned about face.

"I was much better at following a mark than he was. He didn't figure that out during the half an hour that we walked.

"The boy was off duty and there was a neat sign that advised "Self-Service Hours" were in effect when I watched the goon step into the walnut-lined Otis elevator. The car stopped at the sixth floor. I nodded to Tom Geary, the house dick who was perched on the shoe-shine kid's chair, and then followed the tweed jacket up.

"When the doors opened I turned to the right and made a quick case of the doors. Only two had lights shining under them. I checked the other end of the hall: one light on. I knocked. When the door opened I could see well into the room above the petite blonde's page-boy.

"Hmmm…room service is going to get a helluva tip!" she laughed. The left shoulder strap of her chemise slipped as she draped herself against the door and the top of a tear-drop shaped breast was revealed. The silk fabric was held up by what seemed to be a pencil eraser jutting out from behind the material.

"As she shifted her weight back I glanced down. She had tiny, delicately shaped feet. The left one bent up at the joint of her toes and her heel rested against the edge of the door as she came to rest like a beautiful bird on a perch. Her toes were carefully lacquered a bubble-gum pink. It was a cinch that her paint would be a match for a couple of points of interest higher up.

"She stretched slowly, arching her back against the door. It wasn't a big gesture but it was big enough to make sure that I got the message. Page-boy didn't believe in wearing panties.

"Her lips parted and she mouthed "The lobby in thirty," to me then punctuated the invitation with a stab of her soft, pink tongue and a wink.

"The man behind her, dressed in pajama bottoms and tattoos, didn't seem as amused. "Whatayawant?" he demanded.

"Sorry, folks, I guess I got the wrong room," I said

quickly and backed away.

"Too bad," Page-boy said with a sigh and a pout as she was closing the door between us.

"Whataya mean by that?" the voice of Tattoos carried through as the door clicked.

"I crossed to the other end of the hall, glanced along the corridor, then quickly put my ear to the first door. A radio hissed that the station selected had gone off the air. I moved to the next suspect apartment. Muffled voices.

"I took a deep breath and knocked. Nothing happened. I knocked again. Nothing, unless the fact that the voices suddenly fell silent counted as something. I raised my hand and prepared to use my knuckles again just as the door knob began to turn.

"Who the hell – " Tweed let the question die on his thick lips.

"I gave him a broad wink and a smile. "Going to invite me in or should I just wait downstairs?" I asked.

"Tweed's face flushed. "Boss," he said, "this is the guy."

"A man who had been seated in an armchair directly behind the thug at the door stood up. Until he had moved I hadn't seen him at all. He was slight, had thinning blonde hair and a pencil-thin moustache.

"Hello, I am, as has just been pointed out, 'The Guy'," I said. "Or Jud Carson. And you are Jeffrey Brighton. We should talk."

"When Tweed looked over his shoulder at Brighton for instructions I eased forward, slipped past him down the short entranceway and entered the suite's sitting room. Jeffrey Brighton extended a small, fine-boned hand. "I don't believe we have met," he said in a polite tone that spoke of breeding and education. Somewhere in there was the suggestion that he had also been around a lot of bad things in his life. More importantly to me, was the distinct impression that he had done some of them himself and not found it difficult to look in the mirror afterward.

"Brighton nodded once to the man at the door and I could hear the latch set behind me. I moved forward, shook Brighton's hand noncommittally and let the hireling move past me. He took a chair on the other side of the room.

"It is a bit late for callers," Brighton said as he turned to the bar set up on the lowboy. His gesture offered whiskey. Mine accepted and he poured two fingers from a decanter into a pair of glasses. He didn't offer ice. The tweed jacket wasn't drinking.

"You can play cagey all you want," I said, taking a sip. It was decent booze. Not top shelf but not rot, either. "But we both know the game. Your man here saw me with Elaine Merriman tonight." A slight narrowing of his eyes told me that Brighton had never heard the name before. Okay, so it wouldn't be the first time that a client had given me a false moniker. I went on. "I figure that he followed her from her place, picked up my trail, and, well, we all know how that worked out because here I stand drinking your Irish."

"You are here about the letter," Brighton said. He gestured toward the chair behind me and I parked my

* * *

tumbler on the end table, opened my trench coat, thumbed the button on my jacket open and accepted his second invitation. He waited until I had picked up my drink before seating himself across from me.

"That's the nut of it," I agreed as I raised my glass in a salute. "The letter."

\-   *When the Clock Strikes Dead*
Jud Carson, P.I.

*****

"Es regnet," the young woman said as she and Jerome stepped out of the airport terminal and waited beneath the overhang of Tegel airport. He looked at her, did his best, "Sorry, I don't understand" smile and shook his head.

"Raining," she said in English. "It is raining." Then her attention was captured by a young man who strode up to her and swept her up into his arms.

A horn beeped and Jerome looked back to the street in front of him. A hand waved through a half-open window and he moved toward the waiting car.

"How is it going?" Jerome asked as he bundled into the back seat. The driver closed the trunk on his luggage and slid back behind the wheel. Jerome rolled his shoulders and tried to find a comfortable position as the driver pulled smoothly into traffic.

"It has all gone to hell *schnell.* We have her registered at a hotel downtown," Dare said softly to Jud as they settled into the cab and it sped away from the airport stand. He gave the driver an address and gestured towards Jerome's upper lip. "You grew a moustache."

Jerome patted his own stomach and smiled. "And you grew," he smiled. "Where is she really?" He had adopted Dare's whisper in unspoken recognition that even the driver was not to be trusted.

"What makes you think that we have her stashed somewhere else?"

"The fact that you aren't stupid. You already told me that this was going to be a high profile case. You don't want the press hanging around her and snapping pics."

"She's at a house on the outskirts of the city."

"A nice house," Jud offered.

"Yeah, Claire wouldn't have it any other way. She wanted to make sure that there was plenty of room for security and to see anyone coming."

Jud shook his head. "Just who are you expecting?"

"Don't know. It could be radicals. Could be state."

"State?"

"The victim was a government official. You might have noticed that the Soviet Bloc is starting to fall apart like a sugar cube. The Hungarians started taking down their part of the fence in May and then went all the way when they opened the border in August. East Germans poured into Austria.

"I've been watching the news," Jud said, looking out of the window of the Mercedes and watching the city lights speed by. A Mercedes, he thought, they use these for cabs.

"Hard to not be aware of what is going on," Colfield conceded. "But the implications are getting more difficult to figure out."

"Such as?"

"Such as: What happens if this whole thing reaches a critical mass?" He turned to face the P.I. more directly. "What happens if the East Germans decide that they don't want to be 'East Germans' anymore?"

"And just be 'Germans' again?"

Colfield nodded grimly.

"The Kremlin probably wouldn't go for that."

"Not to mention that there is someone out there that actually committed this murder. If they are willing to frame Paula they may be less-than-willing to let her go to trial."

"Any ideas on who that might be?"

"Zero." The lawyer let a wry smile move across his face. "That's why we brought you in, gumshoe."

For a few minutes the two men held their silence. Then, "Claire taking all of this okay?" Jerome asked.

"Claire is Claire," Colfield said. "She takes everything well."

"Even – "

"There is no 'Even'," the lawyer said, cutting him off. "But, I think, even if there were…"

A moment later he went on. "Paula is from the past."

"Long past?"

"Long enough past." They had slipped out of the city and darkness had settled into pools around them. "I knew Paula when I was stationed here. Before I became a lawyer – and a long time before I met Claire."

"So, she's an ex?"

Colfield shrugged and nodded at the same

time, as though he was not too sure himself what his relationship with the woman was or, perhaps, even what it had been.

"Didn't mean to touch a nerve," Jerome said.

"Yeah," Colfield said. "But they do tend to get touched." He took a deep breath and then puffed his cheeks, pursed his lips and exhaled forcefully. "A long time ago," he said, turning his head away from his companion. "Well, it was a long time ago. At least it seems like it was."

"Got it," Jerome said. He started to pat Colfield's arm but held back. "She seems to have been able to get a line on you awfully quick for all of being a shadow of the past."

"Claire and I were in Paris. There was business and after that we were going to just vacation. Paula and I have mutual friends here. It didn't take long."

"And you were in contact with her before the local cops grabbed her," Jerome offered.

Colfield said nothing for a moment and Jerome waited him out.

At last the lawyer replied. "How did you know that?"

"I didn't. Until now."

"You won't say anything to Claire…"

"I wouldn't – but I wouldn't have to," Jerome answered. "But I would put ten to one that she already knows."

The two men were silent for the rest of the thirty minute ride. At the gate to the house grounds a man in a suit stopped them, flicked on a flashlight and, using only the soft side of the beam, illuminated Colfield's face, then Jerome's. He said something in German to the lawyer, who replied in the same language, then he nodded once and stepped back from the car. Jerome imagined he could feel the gun that had been trained on him from the dark being lowered.

"A shibboleth?" he asked.

"It's an old technique," Colfield said. "But still useful."

A moment later the cab halted again, this time at the carriage stop, and the driver turned to them. "This good?" he asked Colfield in American-accented English.

Colfield's head snapped up and his back became instantly erect.

The driver dropped his eyes and seemed to be ignoring the attorney's reaction. "We have an interest in seeing to it that Miss Layman doesn't have any long talks with foreign intelligence operatives," he said.

Colfield leaned forward. "Then get her the hell out of here!"

"And just how are we supposed to do that?" the ersatz cabbie asked.

"Put her in the trunk of this car and drive her to the embassy. Across the border. Somewhere."

"And we explain that to our host nation as what? Don't be ridiculous, Mr. Colfield, you know how this game is played." He glanced at the door into the house as it swung open and spilled light out into the night. "Best pay your fare and be getting along," he said, holding out his hand.

When the Mercedes had pulled away Jerome and Colfield stood under the carriage cover for a moment as the light from the house flooded out toward, but failed to reach, them.

"This place survived the war, huh?" Jerome asked.

"This place survived several wars," Colfield answered.

"What did he mean, 'You know how this game is played'?"

"The U.S. won't protect Paula from the Germans."

"But they don't want her in the hands of a foreign government. So what is the alternative?"

"Well, we can get her out of this mess," Colfield said as they began to cover the few steps toward the open doorway.

"And if that doesn't work?"

"I think they may just kill her."

"Jud! Thank you for coming right away!" Jerome felt his pulse quicken at the woman's voice. The light behind her made her gown seem nearly translucent and brought back a flood of memories and emotion.

"Claire," he said softly, quickening his step and sweeping her into his arms.

Chapter Seven

Her smile was more than a bit crooked; it started as a mere parting of the lips a third of the way from the right side of her mouth, began to open as it neared the center of her cupid's bow and was fully developed when it reached the left side. In another person it might have belied the bearer's sincerity, but Jerome sensed no phoniness. The smile more than reached her eyes. It shone from them. And, despite the unusualness of her expression, it did not detract from her attractiveness; the very unselfconsciousness of her smile enhanced it.

Dare cleared his throat as though he were interrupting a private, and very personal, conversation between them. "Paula," he said, "this is Jud Carson. He's going to be helping us out."

Paula flicked her eyes from Jerome's to Dare's and back again. "Thank you," she said quietly. "I appreciate it."

"Don't be in too big of a hurry," Jerome responded. "You don't know if I am any good at this."

Paula's eyes darted between the two men again. "I know Dare. If he has faith in you, so do I."

Jerome considered for a moment before speaking again. It was clear that Paula was letting him do just that. At last he cocked an eyebrow and leaned in toward her. "Looking at you, I wouldn't guess that you are in the jam that you are. What's there to smile so much about? Or aren't you too concerned about where you are going to be spending the next several years?"

Paula leaned forward as well. "I've been in tough spots before. This isn't my first trip to Berlin and I have a lot of respect for the way that they do things. On top of that, I have a great friend named Dare Colfield and he's made sure that I have great representation. And, not least by any means, he brought you in. If he thought I needed more, he would have gotten me more. Besides, I like to save my tears for when I really need them."

"Mind telling me when those occasions are – just so I know what to look out for?" Jerome asked.

Paula let her smile broaden. "I cry in bed," she said. Then, in answer to Jerome's unspoken question, "When it's really good," she added.

Dare shifted uncomfortably but Jerome held her look without reacting. *She isn't going for a reaction,* he thought. *She's just telling the truth.* "Do you want to tell me what your side of this story is?" he asked after a moment.

Paula's smile faded and she sat back, looking down at her hands. She had clasped them at some point and now they suggested pleading. Her eyes and voice, however, did not waiver or shift. She was confident of herself, if nothing else.

"I was having an affair with Florian – "

"The victim?"

She nodded and twisted her hands back and forth. "Yes. The victim," she said.

You knew he was married?"

Paula smiled again. "Of course I knew that! It wouldn't have been an affair if he hadn't been married!"

"You're pretty easy with that," Jerome said.

"It was an *affair*," Paula said. "This is *Germany*. It isn't exactly news that an older, powerful man would have an affair with a younger woman."

"Okay, but you – "

"I," Paula said, cutting him off, "am not a hypocrite. A lot of people can say a lot of things about me – but they can't say that." She glanced at Dare and Jerome followed her look this time.

Dare shrugged and spread his hands on the table-top. "That's the only way I have ever known her to be," the lawyer said.

"And telling you lies would hardly be in my best interest," Paula went on. "Look," she paused to flip her hair back, "what do I have to gain by not telling you everything that I can to help you? Am I going to save my good name? No. Anybody who has an itch can scratch it on my file. I was sleeping with an older, married man. I've slept with more than one man. I've slept with more than one man at a time, for that matter! I've done a lot of things. But I don't kill. Not the men that I am sleeping with and not anyone else. The idea that I would kill Florian – "

It was Jerome's turn to interrupt – "It was your gun, wasn't it?"

Paula rolled her eyes. "That's what they tell me."

"If you aren't a killer – "

"Why have a gun? Because Florian gave it to me. Because he was concerned that I might need it to protect myself."

"From who?"

Paula shook her head. "Florian was an old school Cold Warrior type. He knew that I had been in intelligence here in Berlin. People like us," she glanced at Dare, "had – have – enemies. With the unrest that is going on Florian thought that it was a good idea for me to have the gun. But I don't care too much for guns."

Jerome made a mental note to ask the lawyer just what he had been up to during his time in Berlin. "Do you know how to use a gun?"

"Of course. I was in the Air Force. Before that I grew up in Montana. My dad was a ranger in Yellowstone. Yeah, I can use all kinds of guns. I still don't like them much."

They considered one another then she went on. "And I can use them very well." Her words had the touch of finality to them as though she felt that the topic had been completely explored and exhausted.

"Tell him about the argument," Colfield said.

"Argument? Let me guess – it was between you and the victim," Jerome said.

Paula nodded. "And with plenty of credible witnesses."

"I'm listening," Jerome offered.

"So were Florian's maid, butler and cook. He wanted to sleep with me."

"The cook?"

"No! Well, yeah," Paula said, "but that's not what I meant. Florian wanted to spend the night in my room. I told him 'No' since his own wife was in the same house. He got angry and we argued."

"Didn't you know she was there before that?"

"She didn't arrive until later," Colfield put in. "She wasn't expected."

"Well that was convenient, wasn't it?"

Paula raised an eyebrow.

"A ready-made reason for murder. If the wife hadn't shown up Paula and the vic would have been trying to set the sheets on fire – " he glanced at Paula, "No offense," he said.

"None taken. Good to know my reputation has gotten around."

"Anyway," he went on, "nobody would have believed she would cap him off if she was in the same bed with him."

"Good point, this does create a weak but possible motive that she wouldn't have had otherwise," the lawyer agreed.

"So why was she there spoiling all the fun?" Jerome pressed.

"I don't know – Florian's nephew brought her because he said she decided to come to the country place. She didn't drive so he did it for her."

"Does he live with them?"

Paula smiled. "Berrin? Not a chance. He was there to show her something – I think it was a book – yeah – he sells books and he came across some antique that he wanted her to see. The next thing we know she is walking into the dining room."

"What was the book?" Jerome asked.

"I don't know – just a book," Paula answered.

"You didn't see it?" Jerome frowned.

"No, things were exciting enough without some antique book to discuss."

"And you didn't sleep with Schumann that night?" Colfield asked.

"Neither one of them," Paula answered.

Jerome studied her for a moment.

"It was a little joke," Paula assured the two men. "I have never slept with Berrin. Only Florian."

"And the next morning he was found dead in his bed."

"Early morning. Like middle of the night morning. And the gun that killed him was found in my dresser drawer."

"No doubt that it is the same gun that he gave you?" Jerome suggested.

Colfield shook his head. "Serial numbers match."

Paula slumped back in her chair and let her chin drop toward her chest.

"You heard the gunshot?"

Paula shook her head. "I didn't hear anything until the local gendarmes paid me a visit."

"Then who – how?"

"The nephew," Colfield answered. "He said that he heard the shot and footsteps running past his door."

"So he claims to have seen Paula?"

Paula shook her head. "No. But he says that he thought the footsteps sounded like they were going toward my room. He is a little hazy on that, though and won't swear to it."

"How did the cops know that you had a gun?" Jerome asked.

Paula shook her head. Jerome turned to Colfield who copied her gesture.

"You don't know?"

"They said that they were informed Paula had a gun."

"Any other guns in the house?" Jerome stood up and stretched. He was beginning to feel the stress of the trip and circumstances.

"Florian had a few. They were checked," Paula

said. "Not that it mattered. The ballistics on mine match."

"I get that," Jerome said. "I'm just trying to figure out who knew you had a gun and why they came to you first."

Colfield drummed his fingers on the table-top and drew their attention. "We aren't going to be able to get around the fact that Paula was sleeping with him, that she knew he was married, and that, by the way, Jud, isn't a major point here in Germany, and that the gun used leads right back to a former Air Force intelligence analyst who was stationed in Berlin. There is just one problem."

"Yeah," Jerome said. "She didn't do it."

When he looked at the woman across the table from him he was pleased to see that Paula's smile returned.

"So now what?" she asked.

"So now we prove it," he said. "But first I get some sleep."

"There's a room ready for you down the hall," Dare said.

*****

Notebook 24, Entry 19

"I'm going to have to trust you – just a little," Brighton said. "I don't want to, but I don't see any other alternative at the moment." He put his glass down and leaned toward me. "Now that Miss 'Merriman'," he said the name carefully, as though trying to make sure that he didn't slip and use another, more familiar one, "no longer has it I suspect that she is desperate to get it back."

"He smiled. "As for you, I don't think that you have any idea whatever about the letter. For all you know it is a letter of credit – or a political plan."

"I nodded. "It could be a party invitation for all I know," I conceded. There was no use in denying it. A question or two at the most would have given Brighton all the evidence he needed that he was right. Besides, as long as he was talking, I was getting smarter. I had no intention of turning the tables.

"I didn't think she would be willing to share that information," he mused. Then, "Well, it is not," he went on. "It is something far more important. And more valuable."

"I looked at my glass and waited until he was ready to go on.

"You've heard of Thomas Jefferson," he began slowly. "He wrote the Declaration of Independence."I nodded. I could have added that the Virginia planter had been pretty heavily influenced by the Swiss jurist Jean Jacques Burlamaqui, but there was no reason to let him think that I was any more educated than the average door knob that he was used to keeping company with. "Two dollar bill," I said.

"Same guy," Brighton agreed with a slight, knowing smile. He figured he had measured my depth and had decided that he wouldn't have to wade too deep to drown me in his intellect.

"I looked at his insurance in the corner. "I got your name. And Jefferson's. He got a handle or does he just respond to whistles?'" The rib-cracker stiffened slightly.

"What's in a name?" Brighton asked, his right hand, palm down gesturing subtly to his companion.

"A. An. Am. Me. Men. Man. Mean." I rattled off the seven words and then turned my attention to the thug again. "Mane. Amen."

"Brighton raised an eyebrow and the corner of his mouth curled and twitched to let me know that he was more annoyed than amused.

"I shrugged. Out of the corner of my eye I could see the too-tight tweed stretch as the man inside of it relaxed in the armchair. The mahaska bulged obscenely even in the low light of the room.

"Brighton picked up the thread of his monologue again. "Jefferson has a lot of fans and a lot of foes. Some of those in each camp have been looking for a particular piece of evidence for a long time."

"The letter," I said.

"The letter," he agreed.

"He nodded and sighed. For a moment he seemed to be considering just how much to tell me. "Jefferson had a slave – a beautiful young woman named 'Sally Hemmings'," he said at last.

"And?"

"And Jefferson may have been a genius and a patriot but he was still a slave owner." He raised an eyebrow again, this time as an unstated question.

"And he was a man," I answered.

"Brighton rocked back and forth slightly in his

chair. "Yes," he said. "And he was a man." He reached into his inside jacket pocket and when his hand reappeared it held a secretary-style wallet. From it he withdrew a piece of yellowed paper. He looked at it with obvious admiration before handing it across to me.

"The image that stared back at me was what poets spend lifetimes trying to describe. I knew that I had about as much chance of putting into words the take-your-breath-away-and-leave-you-happier-for-it-beauty of the young black woman as I would in trying to strike out the Big Bambino, or of going fifteen with Sullivan. I wouldn't even try. Instead I would hope to burn the image into my brain so that when I no longer had the slip of paper I could keep some piece of her in my memory.

"Men, God help me, even men like Jefferson, could be forgiven for being struck by the open, casual, and honest beauty of this long-dead woman. They could not be forgiven for enslaving her for their own desires. I handed the paper back with a mixture of regret and satisfaction. Regret that I could no longer look into the painter's no-doubt poor representation. Satisfaction that slavery was no longer a going concern.

"So, can you imagine," Brighton began, "what would happen if a letter, authenticated to be in Jefferson's handwriting, were to turn up and contain evidence that he had…" it was as though he was doing his best to not discuss the rotting carcass in the parlor.

"Been intimate?" I suggested.

"Fathered children," he answered more directly.

"With her?" I nodded toward the paper he still held.

"With a slave," he said. "It isn't that a white slave owner bedding a slave was so unheard of," Brighton went on. "It's a known fact that Hemmings was Jefferson's wife's half-sister."

"It's that it is Jefferson." I nodded.

"People in both camps would want a letter like that for their own reasons, I thought. The pro-Jeffersonians would want it to show that he didn't let race get in the way of love. And he might have heirs whose mother had been the property of one of the country's most famous founding fathers. His detractors would love to ballyhoo it to diminish his influence. This sin could be used to paint Jefferson as a hypocrite and worse. 'All men are created equal,' and all of that.

"So you can see why it is so important."

"I nodded slowly.

"And you can see why it is so valuable?" This was a question. He wanted to get me involved with the discussion and I wasn't sure that I liked what I thought it meant.

"I sat back, whistled softly then glanced at the over-stuffed tweed in the corner. "Just seeing if you were still awake," I said. "Yeah," I went on, turning back to Brighton. "It would be worth a bunch of two-dollar bills."

"But the best money is going to come from the right people," Brighton said quickly.

"And you know who the right people are," I offered.

"Yes, yes, I do. So you see?"

"See?"

"See why I am willing to pay you – and pay you handsomely, I might add – for your assistance in getting that letter for me. I don't know if your client is simply shopping the article around or prepared to make a deal. And I can assure you, whatever your companion of this evening is offering, I am prepared to offer more than she."

"Things had been going pretty well up till now. I hadn't seen this curve coming and I nearly rolled it when I tried to slam on the brakes. I hoped that my up-raised glass had provided enough cover that he didn't see my surprise at this revelation: He was in the letter *buying* end of the business, not the letter *having*. If he figured that the dame was trying to buy it, too, and was willing to out-bid her, then the question became letter, letter, who's got the letter?

"'I've never made it to the 'handsome' level," I lied. "Just how good does 'handsome' look?"

"Shall we say twenty thousand dollars when the letter is in my hand? And more when I have transacted it with a buyer."

"And how much more would that be?"

"One-sixth of as much as a quarter of a million. Maybe more." He fixed me with his eyes as he waited for a commitment.

"Very well, let's say that," I answered by way of acceptance.

"A capable, resourceful, and wise man. I could have used your talents on many an occasion," Brighton said.

"And don't forget thrifty, kind, reverent and clean,"

I added. "But I don't have it, at least, not right now," I said.

"But you can get it." Brighton was eager now and I could see that his cool, detached manner only went so far. He was a kid at the circus with a fist full of Jeffersons.

"I shrugged and stretched an eyebrow toward the ceiling then let it fall.

"You've been after this letter for a long time," I said.

"A very long time."

"You shouldn't have a problem waiting a little longer," I said as I pushed up from the chair.

"Don't make me wait too long, Mr. Carson," Brighton said. He leaned forward and smiled thinly. "I'd hate to have to reconsider my offer." His eyes flicked to the corner of the room where his goon sat, then they returned to settle on me. "I wouldn't want to start thinking that you are going into business for yourself."

"I picked up my hat from the table and started for the hall.

"Don't bother to get up," I said. "I can find my own way." At the door I turned and twisted the knob, pulled and stepped half-way through the frame. "As far as going into the antique letters business, don't worry – I have enough to do with the business I'm in," I said. "You'll be hearing from me by tomorrow afternoon. Have your money ready. Cash, if you please. And not in two-dollar bills."

-   *When the Clock Strikes Dead*
    Jud Carson P.I.

*****

Someone was hammering.

It's too late for construction, Jerome thought. Why would workers be doing this in the middle of the night? Claire wouldn't be happy. He thought about going down the hall to talk to Dare about it. Then his attention was captured by a new sound.

Someone was cooking. He could hear the bacon sizzling. He breathed deeply and tried to catch the scent but it eluded him. He tossed the covers back, sat up and swung his legs over the side of the bed, his feet moving back and forth until they rested in the slippers there. He stood. It should be colder, he thought. He considered grabbing his shirt but his attention was recaptured by the sound of the frying bacon and he moved from the bedside to and through the bedroom door.

He wondered when they had put a kitchen in his suite. Maybe that was what all the hammering was about. He went to the window and parted the curtains, squinting into the early morning light. He could see the lawn and a simple wire fence on the edge of the property. It looked out of place. Tufts of knee-high grass sprouted here and there on the far side of the fence in sharp contrast to the manicured lawn below his window.

A flutter of movement from below him and to the right caught his eye. Shifting his gaze he could see Claire and Dare seated at a wrought iron table and being served breakfast by a uniformed maid. The table was crowded with mounds of pancakes, platters of eggs, pitchers of juices, and loaves of toast, dripping with butter and jams.

Claire was waiving to him and saying something but he couldn't make out the words because he was too distracted by the fact that she was nude. He knew that he should look away or concentrate on her face; perhaps he could get the message, but he also knew that it was too late. He had missed the chance and now all that he could do was admire her from where he was.

Claire continued to speak but now she was pointing back toward the fence. Reluctantly Jerome shifted his focus away from her. Night had fallen on the far side of the fence and he could only make out the scene by the feeble light reflected from the lawn.

The grass tufts on the other side of the fence were gone and had been replaced by silent, gaunt, and fragile-looking men, women, and children who stared at him with hollow eyes. Their hunger was nearly palpable and he wondered why they did not simply go to the table where Claire and Dare still sat and nibbled absently at the heaps of food on their plates. There was plenty, he thought. Claire and Dare would not begrudge them; they would not even notice the missing food.

He considered going down and cutting through the fence wire, knocking over the posts and inviting the people on the other side to eat until they were full. But even as he imagined the result he discarded it. Not all of those among them were starving; some were strong and full-bodied – and dangerous.

He realized that the people on the other side of the fence weren't simply starving physically. It was a deeper hunger that consumed them. As he watched they began to dissolve; some, he realized with a chill, would disappear forever, others would make their way across the fence. Of them a small number would be the dangerous ones, and, he knew, they would be harder to see when they were on his side of the fence. All of the green on the lawn would disguise them.

The curtain dropped from his hand and he backed away from the window with a sense of dread, bumping into Jud Carson's desk. He moved around the big oak desk and ran his hand over its smooth wood.

It that had been a fixture in a downtown insurance company in the 1940's then moved to the suburbs for thirty years before landing in a furniture store where it had gathered dust for more than a decade. Jerome had rescued it and spent hours cleaning and polishing it when he was stuck for a plot or a turn of phrase.

He looked at the sheet of paper in the Underwood typewriter that dominated the desk. It was a scene with Stan, Jud Carson's favorite cart vendor. He didn't recognize the scene or remember having written it.

"Just 'cause you sits on a horse," Stan said, "don't make you a jockey!" He dipped a ladle-full of fat chili beans and sauce into a bowl and shoved it across the counter toward me without looking up. There was a long drip of chili sauce on the side of the heavy porcelain, terminating at the bottom edge where the bowl curved back toward the smaller diameter of the base. A single drop of red stained the counter top below. Together it equaled an exclamation point.

"Where's the bacon?" Jerome asked.

Stan's head snapped up like the serious end on a

switch-blade. "What the hell you doin' here?" he hissed. "*You* aint' *never* s'pposed to be here!"

"Can you tell me where the bacon is?" Jerome insisted.

Stan's eyes softened. "You have to find your own bacon, young man," he said. Then, "Now git the hell outahere 'fore he shows up and kicks you from here to da' Palisades. An' don' you *never* come back here!"

Jerome turned toward the kitchen, took the few steps across the room and twisted the door handle. The tiled walls were damp with steam and he could see the obscured form behind the shower door. The workmen should never have put a shower in here, he thought. He put a hand out and began to push the sliding door to the right. The spray from the shower head bounced out of the stall and splashed on the floor. Watch your step, he thought as he inched closer. You always have to watch your step.

The shiny black fabric panels of the umbrella met at the apex where a two inch black tip thrust out, pointing at him. It began to move slowly upward and he found himself unable to look away from the tip until the umbrella was held in its more effective position, above the holder's head. The change in position had caused the spray to splash his face and he licked his lips with sudden thirst. The water was salty and made his chest heavy. A lump had formed in his throat.

Gwendolyn Dean smiled from below the umbrella. She seemed to be making room for him in the shower stall and he felt the lump dissolve as the water raced down his cheeks. He ached to reach out for her, to feel her against him, and to press his lips to hers. Gwendolyn continued to smile but he knew that if he moved forward she would move away again. He knew that she was too fast and he was too old to close the gap between them.

Gwendolyn rested the umbrella on her shoulder and began to twirl its handle between her fingers and thumb. She gave him a coy smile and with her other hand she began to unbutton her white cotton blouse.

"Es regnet," she said.

Jerome lost the thread of the dream. He would remember but little of it in the morning.

Chapter Eight

"Acht Bergstrasse, Steglitz." Colfield set back and looked out the windows as the taxi made its way through the streets. The driver did not try to engage him in conversation. His attention remained on the task before him. The ride was smooth and relatively quiet. A few traffic lights inhibited their progress, but only a few and the neighborhoods flicked by quickly.

*****

Jerome looked at the slip of paper in his hand. 'Finnegan's Irish Pub. Colm Costello'. He checked the address again and put it away, pulling out his Berlin street guide. A quick check assured him that he was going in the right direction, and was, in fact, only a few blocks from his destination. He tucked the book back into his pocket and resumed walking.

The late afternoon sun was still warming and the breeze that rustled the tree-lined street was gentle. A car rolled slowly by him and a young couple across the street caught his attention when he heard the girl laugh. Looking their way he watched as she skipped away from her boyfriend's reach. She was tall, as tall as Jerome himself, and could not have reached her twenty-first birthday, he thought. Long, straight, mahogany tresses fell about her shoulders and her light canvas jacket did little to disguise her physical charms. The white cotton skirt that she wore was modest enough but designed for just such a young woman: long of leg and unselfconscious. Her young man was almost as tall as she, with the rail-thin physique of a late-teenager. He wore a black snap-brim tam that reminded Jerome of one he had seen Bob Dylan wearing once.

Jerome chided himself self-consciously. It made no difference that he did not understand their language. He felt as though he were eavesdropping on the young lovers. He knew what they were sharing. With a pang he acknowledged that it was the same thing that he would like to be sharing with Gwendolyn. He lowered his head and picked up his pace. The pub had to be close.

*****

The dark-eyed woman behind the bar flashed him a smile as he entered, then, as if on a switch, toned the greeting down immediately. She didn't become *un*-friendly, she just wasn't *as* friendly. Perhaps she thought I was someone else, Jerome considered. He glanced behind himself just to be sure that no one had followed him in through the open door, and, satisfied that no one had, he covered the few steps to the bar, turned a seat out and looked up and down the length of the pub. He did not see or hear anyone and guessed, rightly, that he had arrived just at the beginning of the establishment's business day.

"Hello," he offered, turning back to the bartender who was working at the sink and still eyeing him with some friendly suspicion. Jerome looked around again. "This is a very nice place," he said.

The bartender washed a glass, plunging it on the boar-bristle brush vigorously, rinsing it, and setting it to dry in the rack. She nodded curtly and picked up another glass.

"When you get a minute," he went on, "I could use a pint of Guinness."

She rinsed her hands, dried them, swept a dark lock of hair back from her face and began to pour from the spigot. The dark liquid, capped with thick foam quickly began to fill the mug. As it neared the rim she pushed the tap back and tipped the glass to let some of the foam escape into the drain. She set the glass aside and returned to the sink. She had washed the remaining few glasses and dried her hands again in a matter of moments. She finished filling the mug with the stout, used the bar knife to skim off the excess foam, finished filling the glass and put it in front of Jerome without another word passing between them. He pushed a bill across the bar and she picked it up, stepped to the register and recorded the sale. She put his change in front of him and smiled professionally when he shoved one of the bills back toward her. She gave him another, albeit small, smile and pocketed the tip before starting to move away.

Jerome lifted the glass, made the gesture of a silent toast to her and drank. He replaced the mug and smiled at her again. "I don't suppose Colm is here?" he ventured.

The woman's eyes, which had seemed a bit friendlier in the last few moments, suddenly became expressionless.

"No," she said flatly.

"Do you expect him to be in soon?" Jerome

pursued. He wondered if a bribe was in order, but realized that he would have no idea how much to offer. Besides, this woman didn't seem to be looking for a bribe. She was looking out for the boss.

"He might be," she said snapping the towel that she held, then, folding it twice, she placed it beside the sink. "Or he might not." She moved to the far end of the bar and picked up a clipboard, busying herself with checking the liquor inventory.

Damn, I'm smooth, Jerome thought. He lifted the mug again and drank. When she turned to count the bottles on the back of the bar he studied her. She was fit without appearing to have spent half her day in the gym. The dark hair fell in waves about her shoulders and her halter top reached strategically just to the top of hip-hugger jeans. The Levi tag meant that they probably cost a bit here, he thought. Or maybe she had a G.I. friend who got them for her at the P.X. Or was it 'B.X.'?

Didn't matter. She was worth it based on looks alone.

With a start he realized that she had stopped her count and been watching him in the mirror before her. He managed to refrain from rolling his eyes but felt his cheeks redden slightly. God, how nice it is to still be able to blush! His lips twitched in a half-smile of innocent guilt and he shrugged. "When you have a minute, I could use another one of these," he said. He drained the mug and sat it down with a satisfied sigh. He let himself hope that he had seen her smile when she turned back around.

*****

Notebook 24, Entry 20

"It was staring at me from the moment that I opened my door. A dead detective had wanted me to have it for some reason. Dixie had made sure that I got it. Now it was time to deal with Danny Granger's box. I poured a drink and pulled the box between the coffee table and couch. On top was a black and white photo of several of us who made our living minding other people's business. Danny Granger had thrown a party when he had moved into his new house with Dixie a few years back. It had been a lot more fun than any of us wanted to admit. We were all a lot younger. There was less blood on our hands. I took a drink and set the photo aside.

"There were case files, Danny's telephone register, his sister's address on a Christmas card that was four years old. The flotsam and jetsam of a private detective's life. At the bottom of the box was a slip of paper. Stapled to it was a pawn ticket for a leather briefcase. It was dated the day before Danny Granger had caught his last case. I picked up the green and black ticket, considered it for a moment and glanced at the clock. Still too early to get across town and see what this final pawn was about. Still, it wouldn't hurt to start getting ready. A shower and a shave, not to mention a fresh suit of clothes, would go a long way toward making me feel human again. It might even take the grit out of my eyes. I stood, dropped the pawn ticket on the table and was turning toward the bedroom when I heard the soft rapping on my door.

"I wouldn't have been too surprised to find any number of people at my door. I more than half expected to find one of the other private dicks who made their living in the city standing there and ready to lay out a plan to settle the score with whoever it had been that ended Danny Granger's career. I wasn't prepared for the one that it turned out to be.

"A moment later Elaine Merriman pushed the hood of her blue velvet cape back and smiled faintly. "Can I come in?" she asked.

"I pushed the corners of my mouth down for an instant and nodded.

"She stepped into the room and paused while I eased the cape from her shoulders. "You'll have to forgive me," I said, pointing to the empty Chesterfield. "It's the maid's year off."

"She turned her head and smiled wanly. "I admire a man who can look after his own needs," she said. "It makes me feel more confident that he can take care of mine."

"I do what I can," I offered.

"She crossed the room, glanced at Granger's box and contents, then turned back to me. "I suppose," she began, "you must wonder why I am here at this hour."

"I shook my head slightly. "I try not to wonder too much, Miss Merriman. I find that it takes the surprise out of life."

"Please, you simply must call me 'Elaine'," she said. She glanced around again and I wondered if she was looking for a place to perch. Then she tossed her head and gave me another strained smile. "Well, the fact is, after you left, I saw a man follow you. I wasn't sure, of course, that isn't my line of work, but I was pretty sure. So – "

"So you came here to warn me," I said.

"She bit her lower lip and nodded. "You must think me very silly, Mr. Carson."

"Not at all, Elaine," I said, crossing to her. "And please, you simply must call me 'Jud'."

"We stood facing each other for a moment. Then, "There is something else that I was wondering about," she said.

"What is that?"

"How it would feel to kiss you," she said. Then her chin tilted to just the right kiss-me angle and her breath was on my mouth as I descended to answer her curiosity.

"For several minutes we busily satisfied our interests. At last I stepped back and let my arms release their hold on her willing body.

"And?" I asked.

"And I am glad that I caught you when I did," she said, one hand touching her hair and the other smoothing her dress. "It looks as though you were getting ready for bed and if I had arrived any later it would have been very embarrassing for me to leave here several hours from now."

"I don't know, I have a very understanding landlord," I said.

"Good night, Jud," she said, leaning forward for a final kiss.

"I locked the door after her and headed for the shower. I was going to have to postpone my trip to the pawn shop or find another way to get that errand seen to."

- *When the Clock Strikes Dead*
Jud Carson, P.I.

*****

This is not the kind of trip I had planned, Colfield muttered to himself as the taxi cruised through the late afternoon. He and Claire were supposed to be on vacation with a little work thrown in. After the business meetings in Paris they were to have three day break with nothing to care for other than one another. Another three days would be spent judging moot court, and, since this had been his first invitation to do so, his last-minute withdrawal would probably mean that it would be his last as well.

He turned his thoughts to more important and pressing issues. He had tried, and, to a limited extent succeeded, in creating an emotional distance between Paula and himself. He and Claire had engaged the best criminal defense attorneys that they could get, but the very best were not available at any price. Florian Schumann had been an important and influential man. Few wanted to be associated with Paula's defense. It had quickly become apparent that they would have to take charge of the case if there were to be any chance of exoneration.

Claire had summed it up, "You have to call him," she had said the day after they arrived in Berlin. "He doesn't play by the rules."

Colfield had contacted Jud Carson the same day and arranged for him to join the team. He sighed. Well, he thought, to be around the team, anyway. He knew from experience that Jud Carson was not a team player. He shrugged it off. No matter how unorthodox, he had to admit, Carson did get results. And he owed the detective.

He turned his attention to the part of the effort that he was supposed to be an expert at. Although German courts could no longer impose the death penalty there was still life imprisonment. Typically that would mean about 15 years before the option of parole came up. Life enough, he thought. Sometimes, if the court was looking to make a statement the convicted could be looking at closer to 20 years before being allowed parole. And this case would be just the right kind for that type of treatment. A senior statesman being bedded by an American femme fatale who just happened to be ex-military intelligence. This would be a perfect story for the papers. And a nightmare for everyone involved.

He glanced at his watch. What was he thinking, calling Carson and getting him into this? No matter what his qualifications, they were State-side. Here he wasn't licensed, didn't have any contacts and didn't even know the language. Colfield wasn't sure, but he didn't think that the detective even knew how to manage the bus and subway system. It was wrong of him to have called Carson. It had been a knee-jerk reaction. A woman that he cared for was accused of murder; call for Jud Carson and put the hard-hitting P.I. to work. Déjà vu. But this wasn't back-water Benton. This was Berlin. He may have had reason to overcome the lack of skilled police back home. Not so here in the FRG – they had skilled investigators and plenty of them.

He tried to console himself that Claire had declared calling Jud an obvious decision that had to be made, just as she had the first time that the three of them had met, but he had to admit that he had already planned to convince her of the need to call the detective if she hadn't taken the lead. Now he had painted himself into a corner without a window. Carson was here and wouldn't take a bum's rush back to the States.

*****

The two men entered the bar from opposite directions. The combination of events nearly caused Jerome to drop the freshly-filled mug of Guinness.

The man coming from the kitchen had a broad smile, glasses, and the look of a man who knew how to handle himself. His smile spread as he looked past Jerome toward the doorway. Jerome could hear someone moving there. He shifted his gaze to the mirror but the barmaid was blocking his view of the door. The man from the kitchen placed a box on the corner of the bar and moved around it as he made his way past Jerome, a hand outstretched to shake and the other raised in an invitation to a brotherly hug.

"Colm!" Dare Colfield said. Jerome could hear back slapping behind him. He relaxed and finished his stout.

"Dare!" the barman said, an Irish lilt in his voice. "It's been too long!"

Jerome put the mug down and sat back. The barmaid was smiling at Colfield from her position behind the bar. As he watched she seemed to remember that he was present and the smile dropped. She turned her eyes on him and he could see the concern there. She began to move toward the end of the bar. Jerome could sense the protective nature of her relationship with Colm despite his having what seemed to be at least a dozen years on her.

I wouldn't want to tangle with her because she considered me a threat to him, Jerome thought. He said nothing, waiting, letting the greetings and introductions play out without his assistance.

The barmaid whispered something quick and urgent to Colm in German and managed to put herself between him and Jerome at the same time.

"Jud," Colfield said, putting a hand on Jerome's shoulder, "I want you to meet an old friend, the host of the house, and the proprietor, Colm Costello. And this is the finest barmaid in Berlin, Daisy. Colm, Daisy, this is an old and good friend of mine, Jud Carson."

Jerome tried to stand but found his way still blocked by the barmaid. He was pleased and relieved to see that the cloud had lifted from her eyes and she was smiling. He put his hand out and she took it in hers. "I am very glad to meet, you," she said in her Irish-German accented English. "Any friend of this one's," she tilted her head toward Colfield, "is a friend of the house."

"It's my pleasure," he answered. She let him hold her hand for a moment longer, then, keeping eye contact, eased out from between her boss and him.

"I've heard a lot about you," Colm said, shaking Jerome's hand and gripping his forearm with the other. "It's a pleasure to have you here."

"I'm just sorry that it had to be under these circumstances," Colfield said.

"True, true," Colm agreed. For a moment the three men studied their shoes. Daisy slipped back behind the bar and Jerome noticed that she was still wearing a bit of a smile. He couldn't tell if it was from relief or amusement.

"Colm," Colfield began, "I was thinking that you might let us pick your brain a bit about this situation."

Colm made a face as if to say 'I don't know what good it will do' but shrugged and moved back around the bar. "But I think we need something to study on," he said. He lined up three shot glasses.

"Powers," Colfield said.

"Ah, and me as well," Colm said. He turned his eyes to Jerome.

"I've gotten rather fond of Tullamore Dew."

"And so it is," Colm said. He turned to the back bar, grabbed the two bottles and an instant later had poured the three doubles. Daisy moved across the bar room floor with an empty tray and began to collect empty glasses there.

Colfield lifted his glass and saluted his companions. "Sláinte!

"Prost!" Colm responded, raising his as well.

"Here's mud in your eye," Jerome added.

The three men drank as one.

*****

A week in Berlin had made Jerome more comfortable with the people, places and transportation. It had not made him feel more optimistic about Paula's impending trial. Colfield had managed to slow the wheels of the German legal system by using the force of Claire's wealth and Paula's home-grown girl hero status to rope the U.S. State Department into making at least a tacit show of interest.

The lawyer had brought pressure to bear on the defense counsel to file enough motions to keep the proceedings from proceeding too quickly and had demanded that potential witnesses Frau Schumann and Herr Berrin Schumann return from the free FRG to the occupied American zone of West Berlin for more detailed depositions. Both had balked and the court was reluctant to act as yet; the widow was, officially, grieving, and the nephew was, officially, engaged in delicate contract negotiations for his employer.

If it was not rapid progress at least it was not rapid defeat. Jerome had taken to putting in evenings at Finnegan's where Daisy was spending more time at his end of the bar and, of late, asking about San Francisco and what it might have to offer a young woman like her. Her smile was quicker and her eyes seemed to seek him whenever he was in the pub. He had resisted mentioning the *Saffron* so far.

"You could use a drink," Colm Costello said. "Powers for me. And yourself?"

Jerome sighed. "I'm still partial to Tullamore Dew," he said.

The Irishman straightened, turned, poured, and placed the glasses in a matter of practiced, graceful moves that took only seconds. "Can't get that so easily in Ireland," he said, gesturing toward the paler whiskey in the glass in front of Jerome with the glass of darker Powers whiskey in his own. "It gets exported."

Jerome lifted the glass and swirled the liquid.

"To what shall we drink?" Costello asked.

"To freedom?" Jerome suggested.

"Ah, a lovely thing to choose," the barman responded. "To freedom it is."

The two men upended their glasses and set them quietly on the bar between them.

"You look to have troubles enough for two men," Costello offered.

"It's a stumper," Jerome conceded.

Costello put his elbows on the bar and leaned across until his whisper could reach Jerome's ear without effort and, equally importantly, without giving others the opportunity to listen in on their conversation. "And would it have anything to do with a certain American woman who is in dire trouble?"

Jerome nodded. He toyed with the glass in front of him. "I don't see how to get her clear of this," he said. "Ballistics says that the bullet was fired from her gun. She had the gun."

"But you believe her when she says that she didn't use the gun?"

Jerome nodded.

"Could she have been drugged, or," Costello tipped the empty glass before him. He left the question unasked.

Jerome shook his head. "Clean and sober for a couple of years. No reason to believe that she fell off the wagon just long enough to commit murder and then go back to the straight and narrow without a shiver or a shake."

"Do you mind if I ask a technical question?" Costello asked.

"As long as it isn't too technical," Jerome answered.

Costello poured two more drinks. "Could be thirsty work," he offered. When the bottles were returned to their places he began to lean back again, but was interrupted by a group of men who had just entered the bar. The three shared a quick and friendly greeting in German that mostly eluded Jerome but must have included the men's drink order because Costello pulled a small serving tray from above the bar and began to fill it with glasses.

"Go about your business," Daisy said. Her Irish-accented English tinged with a German undertone still captivated Jerome and made him wonder who she had learned the language from. She deftly began to fill the glasses. For a moment she stood quietly while she waited for the foam to settle on a Guinness draft. Her dark eyes darted around the room and came, at last, to Jerome's. A smile like sunrise flashed over her face and then she returned her attention to the task before her.

"I'm so lucky that she lets me work here," Costello smiled as Daisy started around the bar. She came to stand beside Jerome as she picked up the tray.

"Don't get too comfortable," she said, giving Jerome a wink. "I t'ink I can get two for the price of you, Colm Costello!"

Jerome watched her move away, allowing himself to enjoy the view until Costello cleared his throat and reclaimed his attention.

"That question that I had," Costello went on.

Jerome nodded.

"Well, it's about the weapon itself. Would it be a revolver or is it an automatic?"

"Automatic," Jerome answered.

Costello nodded and 'hmm'ed' to himself. "I thought that it might be. You know, I had a friend once who was quite a pistol shot – he was known far and wide – and one day he was challenged to a shooting match." Costello sipped from his glass and Jerome did the same.

"There's a story here, isn't there?" Jerome asked.

"Maybe so, maybe so," the barman answered. "Now, it would hardly be a fair match if the two men were using different types of guns, so they agreed to the make and caliber and set the date. But things didn't go smoothly."

"They never do," Jerome noted.

"True, true," Costello went on. "You see, the night before the match my friend had let his son clean his gun. And on the day of the match my friend had a problem. When they got to the shooting range he found that his son had done a fine job of cleaning the pistol, but he had neglected to put the barrel back in place."

Both men sipped.

"Can you imagine?" Costello went on. "How can you have a match without a barrel in the gun?"

"So your friend forfeited?"

"Ah, no, not a bit. After the challenger had taken his shots, he took out the barrel from his gun, cleaned it, and my friend put it in his gun."

"And it fit?" Jerome asked quietly, sitting up and squaring his shoulders.

"Well, certainly," Costello said with a smile. "Thanks to your Mr. Ely Whitney. Interchangeable parts, you know." He tossed off the last of his Powers and washed the glass in the bar station beside him, putting the glass to drain.

"Thank goodness the two of them used

different targets," Costello went on. "If not, even an expert wouldn't be able to tell the difference in the bullets – fired down the same barrel, you know. They all had the same markings."

Jerome shuddered.

"So, what do you think of that little story?"

"I think that I could use a long talk with your friend," Jerome said.

Costello picked up a cloth and began to polish the bar. "Well, that won't be possible," he said. "For you know he disappeared right after that little shooting match. Hasn't been seen for many a year by any who could call his name. Went the way of the pixies. Or so I am told."

Jerome watched him for a moment before responding. "I wonder if there is another expert that I could talk to."

"No one on this side of that wall is going to be willing to talk about something like this. Or, if they did, you could be sure that they would make an appointment with the polizei right afterward. Maybe before, as well." The barman dropped his voice. "You'd need to talk to someone on the other side. Someone who is used to working with – that sort of thing."

"Good thing I have a passport," Jerome said. "I wonder what else I would need."

"Well, you would certainly need a passport. And Money," Costello went on. "And strong nerve. And more than a little luck."

"Well, I'm told that money is not an obstacle. And I have always had more luck than sense." He finished his drink. "Seems to have made up for nerve."

"Well, now that's the thing, you see."

Jerome settled back to wait for the bad news.

"You see, if you were to use your passport and go through to the other side of the looking glass, as it were, you would not be traveling alone," Costello frowned.

"I wouldn't?"

Costello shook his head sadly. "No, no you wouldn't. You would have a whole line of police and soldiers and spies – " he shook at the thought "and they would all be behind you and around you and taking down notes on when you crossed the border and what street you went up and which way around what corner and – "

"And who I talked to?"

"Oh my, yes, they would certainly want to know who you talked to," the barman agreed. "That they certainly would, and make no mistake, Jud Carson – they have ways of finding out. And, of course, *what* you talked to them about. That would be important to them."

"So it would be better if I were to find another way across the border."

Costello blew a gust of air and nodded. "That it would, indeed."

"And you could tell me how to do that."

"Well, it's a border, but it isn't so much of a challenge getting to the East, you see," Costello met Jerome's eyes, "as it is getting to the West. Of course, it is a kind of an open city at the same time that it is surrounded and occupied. If no one knows you've gone East, then there's precious few looking for you to be coming back West."

"I think I am going to need another drop,

Colm," Jerome said.

"And I think that I am going to have another myself. Just don't tell the boss, eh?"

Chapter Nine

Daisy smiled. Jerome recognized that this lifting of the muscles around her mouth was not the same as when she was greeting returning patrons, or even the one that she gave her employer. It warmed him and he basked in it before feeling the cold jab in his chest that told him what her smile was reminding him of. Gwendolyn Dean's smile ghosted in his mind and he lowered his eyes from Daisy's. When he looked up again she had turned away and was totaling bar tabs. Behind her Colm entered from the small room that contained the dart board and two teams who were doing their best to damage the walls and preserve the boar-bristle board that the barman had spirited from his former pub.

"Jesus," Colm muttered softly as another dart thunked into the wall. "I think you should come with me," he said as he passed by Jerome. The two men moved to the back of the pub and into an enclosed booth. Colm shut the door behind them and took his seat across from Jerome. He folded his hands on the table and shook his head slowly from side to side. "They don't have to be John Lowe but it would be nice if they didn't destroy the room every time they come in." He grimaced and seemed to shake the image away. "So, here we are. I've come up with a name and a place and a time." He slid a slip of paper across the table to Jerome but left his hand on top of it.

"I'm going to tell you now – I don't know how safe this is going to be. You'll have to cross over the wall and when you are over there you are on your own."

"How much on my own?" Jerome asked quietly.

"Lad, this is a war zone. Just because they aren't shooting tonight doesn't mean that they aren't going to be shooting in the morning. And, for that matter, just because you don't hear them shooting doesn't mean that they aren't using silencers. You'll be on your own." He tapped the piece of paper with his fingers. "And you are going to go there to talk about guns and how they can be used to commit murder," he pointed out.

"This guy that you are sending me to, do you trust him?" Jerome asked.

Colm smiled wryly. "You're using the word 'trust' in Berlin? More than that – in *East* Berlin?"

"I get it," Jerome said.

"This man," Colm tapped the paper again, "he can be trusted just as far as it is in his interest to be trustworthy. If he decides that he is better off turning you in, he will. And he will make up anything that he decides he needs to."

"Does he speak English?" Jerome asked.

The barman nodded. "Very well educated. A thick accent, but easily understood. Language won't be the problem."

The two men looked at one another for an instant then both looked away.

"Are you still interested?" Colm asked at last.

Jerome nodded. "How much?" he asked.

"He says five hundred," Colm answered.

"Marks?"

"Dollars."

"That's not much. No problem," Jerome said.

"It's a large sum to those in the East," Colm said. "And it is a real problem. You can't carry that into the East."

"Then how – ?"

Colm reached into his trousers pocket and pulled out a small metal object. It was black, smooth, and oval. It appeared to have been well-used. The dull paint was rubbed and even chipped away in some places. He carefully unscrewed it to reveal the hollow compartment within. He placed the two halves on the table between them.

"If you are caught with this you are going to have some serious problems," Colm said.

"Oh, crap," Jerome said.

*****

Wido Vogt eased the edge of the curtain back with the long, thin fingers of his left hand. With his right he steadied himself against the window frame. Filmy, pale gray eyes scanned the street but little registered. His sight had been failing for years and he knew that it was only a matter of time, a few years, more likely less, before the last rays of light illuminated his life. He hoped again that he would be dead before he was blind. A lifetime of beloved work hung on the walls of the small, dingy apartment overlooking Karl-Marx-Allee in the Friedrichshain section of his native East Berlin. Just a little further to the east, past Warschauer Strassee, the thoroughfare became Frankfurter Allee. An address there would be less impressive.

His photographs of the righteous worker's

struggle had been his ticket to a few minor comforts and a few small considerations over the decades. And there had been other services to the state beside the use of a camera.

Vogt had weathered regime turn-overs and watched colleagues lose their influence with the gray men who controlled his world. Many had simply gone away, never to be heard from, or of, again. Others remained but had never been the same after being questioned by the Stasi. Vogt remained. Vogt had been strong. Vogt had known who to trust and whose trust to gain. And he had known when to betray their trust.

The old man shuffled into the small kitchen and put the kettle on to boil. He had a bit of strong black tea left and it would be just the thing on a chill and damp evening, he thought. He took down the plain white tea cup and placed it carefully on the table. Hannalore had enjoyed having tea with him. No, no, I mustn't think of her, he told himself firmly. Hannalore had been gone far too long to think about now. He scooped tea from the tin and put it in the cup.

He stood by the stove and let the open flame warm him while he waited. Hannalore had never been in this apartment, he mused. His mind still held her image: a strong, vibrant woman just past her twenty-seventh birthday. Clear green eyes and honey-blond hair that fell like a water-fall to her shoulders. When he met her she had not suffered yet. He liked to think of her that way. Before.

The kettle began to whistle and he switched off the gas. He poured the water carefully and put the kettle back on the stove, but on a cold burner. He sometimes forgot and it made feeble attempts to muster the energy for a true whistle. That reminded him of things he would prefer, and be better off, he admitted, to forget.

He sat down at last to let the tea steep. Hannalore would not be denied. She was before his eyes. She was alive and strong and smiling her encouragement. They had been so young. They had been so sure that they were doing the right thing.

She had watched in open awe as his strong, quick and clever fingers did their work. He could repair a clock. Or a camera. Or a gun. Vogt moaned the name of his one love. He had learned the painful lesson that resistance to the Soviet liberators and the East German patriots was foolish and futile. When he was ordered to identify Hannalore's body, broken and disfigured, he had known that he would never again involve himself in trying to re-unite the partitioned Germany. He would work to create the worker's paradise. He would dedicate his efforts to freeing and uniting the oppressed wage slaves of the world. And, if necessary, he would report on those who would threaten the state. Or Wido Vogt.

*****

It's no more dangerous than walking down on the waterfront after sundown, Jerome told himself again. He had memorized the name and address then destroyed the slip of paper that Colm Costello had given him. A separate note had detailed the instructions for travelling into East Berlin and, more importantly, for getting back out again after his meeting with the East German.

Jerome had imagined a midnight crossing at

the infamous Checkpoint Charlie; he would pull the brim of his fedora low over his eyes to cut the glare of the searchlights and the collar of his trench coat up against the damp air. The American sergeant would check his passport, give him a stern reminder that he would be traveling behind the Iron Curtain, and wish him good luck.

He could see himself walking across the no-man's land from the West into the East, his shoes smacking wetly against the rain-slicked pavement. The silhouette of a Soviet Army soldier, helmeted, AK-47 slung over his shoulder stood before him. Others in machine-gun turrets were stationed in the concrete towers flanking the most famous border crossing in the world.

It had taken Colm only a moment to disabuse Jerome of his imagined crossing.

Jerome would take a bus to the UBahn station, transfer and leave the subway stop on the eastern side of the wall, walk a few blocks and then enter the apartment building on Karl-Marx-Allee. There was an elevator but it would probably be out of order. The stairs would have to do.

He was expected but there was really no way to know what he should expect. He might be met by East German guards as soon as he stepped foot on the platform beyond the wall. He might be followed and the apartment raided while he was there. It was possible that the man he was going to see would not be the real resident, but, rather a Stasi agent. The man might have sold him out to the Soviets and he might be arrested after the meeting. In any case, if the money or the container that it was in was discovered, he would be detained. The Communists would certainly charge him with smuggling and probably espionage as well. He would have to make certain that he left the capsule on the eastern side. It was valuable, but it would be retrieved later by someone else. Jerome shuddered to think of the implications of that information.

"And this is the best idea we have?" Jerome asked.

"Well, there are worse ideas," Colm countered.

"Would you do this?" Jerome studied the other man's face. He knew that Costello had a past that he did not care to discuss, at least not with people he had known for as short a time as he had known Jerome. That he was vouched for by Colfield meant a great deal but not that much. Still, Jerome was confident that the barman was not about to send him into the mouth of hell for no good reason at all and with no chance of success.

"I do it about half a dozen times a year," Colm said. "This just isn't my month. And I sure as hell wouldn't use one of those eggs to get the job done!"

*****

Jerome felt the train lurch forward. In a moment or less he would be crossing, illegally, into East Berlin. If a soldier or conductor decided to challenge him the entire plan would fall apart before it had a chance to get underway. He willed himself to relax, but the vibration of the train was amplified by the secreted container and he tightened his belly reflexively.

The young woman sitting across from him glanced up and smiled. She tapped her foot, presumably in time to the music playing on her Walkman. Jerome let his eyes glide over her and fixed on the tunnel that flashed by outside the train's windows.

The train came to a halt before he had managed to relax. When the doors slid open he expected to see his nightmare become reality. But no soldiers, police or ticket takers boarded. The doors swooshed closed again and the train was in motion once more. Two more uneventful train stops followed and he began to relax when the train came to a halt again. He read the station name and took a deep breath. Just as he began to stand he noticed that the young woman opposite him was doing the same. Her earphones were still perched on top of her short dark brown hair. The Walkman was still playing.

She smiled at him again and moved toward the door. Jerome hesitated then felt the panic rush over him. Was she following him? She had seemed to be quite ready to go on until he had stood up. Suddenly she, too, was getting off the train at this particular station. Should he go on to the next stop and double back? Should he try to cross the station and return to the West? He glanced at the girl again. She seemed to be moving very slowly toward the open doors. If he had felt fear before it turned to near-panic when she turned back toward him. She smiled. She winked. She stepped through the doors and stood waiting for him. She pursed her lips and, thrusting her pelvis and breasts out, put her right hand on her hip and blew him a kiss.

Jerome moved toward the door as the tone sounded to warn travelers that the train was preparing to leave the station. He allowed himself a smile and let some of the tension of the past minutes escape in a sigh. The girl was no Soviet spy. She was just a working girl. He shook his head as he neared her and she raised an eyebrow as if to ask "Are you sure?" He shook his head again and eased past her. He didn't need a hooker right now. He needed a drink. And a bathroom.

*****

Notebook 24, Entry 21

"I looked at the note again. She had a firm, graceful script that could have been lifted from an engraver's folio; the blue ink staining the ivory note-paper with carefully controlled strokes and gentle flourishes spoke of business and intimacy at once. The faint aroma of jasmine laced the paper, unnoticeable if you didn't hold the note close and breathe deeply.

"After a moment I shook my head and dropped the note of fluid azure pen-strokes and scented jasmine ivory to the blotter on my desk. I stared at it for a moment, then, with a tight smile that told my empty office that I was in control of me, I took the nickel-plated cigarette lighter from my desk, flicked it to life and held the hungry flame to the edge of the note paper.

"I was under no delusion that my office was safe from prying eyes and lock picks. Jeffrey Brighton knew who I was and I wasn't going to leave him any clues as to where I was going.

"When the blackened corner had curled and the

flame raced upward to the tip that I held pinched between index finger and thumb I turned the sheet to make sure that all of the writing had been consumed. Satisfied, I dropped the ash and single remaining scrap of paper into the trash can beside my desk, watching to make sure that it went out.

"For all of the emotion that she had brought up in me, the message itself had been simple: she wanted to meet me at the *Bourbon and Branch* at one-thirty. I didn't like the idea of going back to the same place but there wasn't enough of a reason to argue against it. Maybe it was on her way to her next stop. Maybe it was close to where she was going to be earlier in the night. Maybe she thought the lighting made her look better. I doubted the last: I was willing to bet that she knew how to look like a million bucks anywhere.

"The fact that I wouldn't be able to get a message to her now to change the meeting place clinched it. I was going to be making another trip to the place that had been a safe speak-easy throughout the Prohibition years.

"Before I made my way back to the tables in the red-flocked dining room of the *Bourbon and Branch* I took a detour to the waterfront. Stan was perched like a bird of prey on a stack of crates behind his steam table. The racing form in his hand was stained and I could see circles and strike-outs on the side that faced me. He tapped a pen against his temple as he studied the page before him like a fiancée considering a collection of engagement rings.

"You're never going to hit the long shot so you might as well give it up," I said.

"Look who's talking," he snorted. "You been lookin' for the big pay-off long as I knowed you." He didn't stir from his seat.

"And see how well I've done?" I made my way behind the steam table and reached below the counter for a cardboard cup. I filled it with chili from the steamer and popped a lid on it. I stuck a plastic spoon in my coat pocket and fished out a five. Taking the cigar box from the shelf beside Stan I flipped it open and dropped the bill inside. The .38 was conspicuous in its absence.

"Where's the roscoe?"

Stan shifted his skinny carcass on his perch. "Got stole." He seemed to hesitate as though he were going to look at me, then he shook his head and circled something vigorously on the form. "I gits another one tomorrow."

"He was lying. No one was going to walk away after stealing from Stan. Times were hard and he had hocked his protection. Stan was known to be a shooter. The odds on someone trying him were slim. The odds on someone trying him without a gun were zero. I pulled the chrome-plated .45 automatic from my pocket and put it on top of the five.

"Two bucks," he said without looking up from his form.

"Yeah," I said. "It's been two bucks forever." I closed the box without taking anything out.

"Grab some napkins," he went on.

"You telling me that you're getting generous?" I asked. I grabbed some of the thin, wheat-colored paper napkins and stuffed them on top of the spoon in my coat. Picking up the cardboard container of chili I stepped around the end of the counter and started off into the darkness.

"I'm telling you that you is a slob," Stan said.

"Hope your horse breaks a leg," I said as the fog enveloped me.

"See you tomorrow."

- *When the Clock Strikes Dead*
Jud Carson, P.I.

*****

The streets of East Berlin were strangely empty, though not quite devoid of people, when Jerome emerged from the subway station. A few here. A few there. More tension mounted within him as he ran the directions in his head yet again. A left, a few blocks, a right, a few blocks, a number, a few flights. He did not hesitate or look around for landmarks. To do so could easily tell others that he did not know his way around; he was a stranger; he did not belong. And that could prove more than embarrassing. It could be fatal.

His footsteps echoed slightly as he made his way. The few people on the street did not turn to look at him, but he felt that he was being studied nonetheless. It's like an episode of *The Twilight Zone*, he thought. He consoled himself that he did not see anyone in uniform on the street, but that would mean little. All of his life he had been told that the Soviet Bear turned its subjects into informers. Anyone and everyone was suspect.

He made the first turn and allowed himself a small sigh. A more residential and less industrial street stretched before him. Two more streets and another turn. He heard the footsteps, unhurried but measured, behind him. He pressed his lips together in a tight seal and felt the veins in his temples pound. One more street. The footsteps continued. He managed a glance at the first floor windows beside him, spotting first his, then the image of the person behind him. An older man with a grocery bag and a small, black cap. A worker, Jerome guessed. He allowed himself a deeper breath.

The right turn. An instant later he realized that he had forgotten the street number of the building he sought. He slowed down. It would not be a good thing to begin walking up and down the street while he hoped to remember. The footsteps, still measured and still unhurried, were behind him again.

He glanced at the windows beside him again. Gone was the man's black cap. Gone was the grocery bag. Gone was the worker. An East Berlin cop was half a block behind him. Jerome could hear the word "Halt!" in his mind. Distracted, he had moved closer to the building beside him and his right shoe brushed against the concrete stoop. He looked at the doorway beside him and swallowed hard. The street number connected with that on the slip of paper that Colm had shown him. He stepped up and pressed the second door bell. The door buzzed instantly – his host was waiting for him, he realized with a silent prayer of thanks, and he pushed through. He by-passed the elevator in favor of the stairs at the end of the foyer. The door had closed with a loud clack behind him and he allowed himself a glance toward it as he made the turn of the first landing. The cop had continued past the building with the same measured and unhurried pace.

"You walk too slow," Wido Vogt said as he closed the door behind Jerome. He pointed to the armchair in the far corner of the small room. "Sit," he said.

"Aren't you going to lock the door?" Jerome asked.

Vogt snorted as if to say, "A locked door means nothing here." He put the kettle on the stove and lit the flame. "You have something for me from my friends?"

"Yes," Jerome said, standing again. "I can get it for you," he said. He looked around for the bathroom. "It will only take a minute."

Wido Vogt waived a hand toward a doorway beside Jerome. A pale green curtain was stretched across the opening and Jerome lifted it, slid into the small bedroom, nearly bumping into the bed, and turned to his left. The bathroom, sparse and functional, was lit by a low-watt bulb.

Despite his urgency to be rid of his cargo, Jerome found it more difficult than he had imagined to remove. When it emerged at last he eased it from the latex condom. Then he placed the container in the sink and flushed its wrapper away. He scrubbed and dried his hands with the slightly gray bar of soap and dried his hands on the slightly gray towel that hung beneath the light fixture.

The tea was ready when he returned to the sitting room. Wido Vogt had prepared a service and placed it on the table beside the chair he had indicated to Jerome.

He did not look up when Jerome entered. "Put it there," he said, pointing to a shelf that held a small radio and a time-faded photograph of a couple that Jerome suspected included a much younger version of his host. He placed the cylinder on the shelf and turned back. The old man was busy not looking at him.

"Nice place," Jerome offered.

"Hmph! Is a dump. But is paid for by glorious state for the use of useful and grateful citizen. Windows do not open and there is no fan. Sweat like useful pig. Windows leak and is no heat. Freeze like glorious Soviet bear." He looked up and fixed Jerome with a pale, steady eye. "Sit. Tell me why you are here."

Jerome perched on the faded chair and gave the old man the highlights of the story, leaving out the particulars which he felt would not further the purpose of getting him done, getting him out, and getting him back to the land of the sacred secret ballot.

When he was finished he sat back, sipped at the black tea and waited.

"For this Irish sends to me," Wido Vogt sighed as if to say that his time was not only wasted but that his ancestry was being insulted at the same time.

"He seemed to think it could be barrel switching," Jerome said. His eyes flicked to the clock on the wall. He had already been here longer than he had anticipated and his nerves were beginning to fray.

"Hmph," Wido Vogt sounded. "Irish will tell me how to play cello next. Of course it was barrel which is moving from weapon to weapon. But – and here is real problem – so what? Bullets match barrel. Barrel is now back in woman's gun. Polizei make arrest of woman and polizei are happy."

"Doesn't sound too hopeful," Jerome said.

"What does American know of hope?" Wido Vogt asked. The question was quick and the words were sharp but the voice was soft. "For Americans every day is hope fulfilled. Go. Come. Have. Throw away. Hope is *not* having hope fulfilled. This is to *have* hope." He sipped his tea, sat back, crossed his hands across his chest and closed his eyes. Jerome feared that the old man was nodding off and he felt the urge to return to the small bathroom.

"There is a way," Wido Vogt said, his eyes still closed.

Jerome leaned toward the old man.

"Must find out who first."

"Who?"

"Who has killed the old man. Then, perhaps, not so hard to prove how."

"I'm listening," Jerome coaxed.

"You must find out who has done this thing," Wido Vogt went on in the same casual manner. "Then, search and find weapon that matches woman's. This will be the one that was used."

"What if they threw it away?"

The old man shook his head. "Not so easy to do. What if it is found? This could be most embarrassing. And guns – even in the free West – must be accounted for. If one becomes missing there are questions. No, he will have the gun still. Besides, he has what reason to hide? He is not suspect. The gun used is in hands of polizei – we know because polizei say so and polizei are never wrong. No, he has gun that he has used for this thing."

"So, if I manage to figure out who did it? What

then?"

A slow smile began to steal across Wido Vogt's lips. "You listen. That is good. Now comes the reason that the Irish sends you to me."

Chapter Ten

Back. In the West. Jerome watched the lights flicker by as the taxi sped away from the subway station and back toward the refuge of the estate that Clair and Dare had made their base. He looked at the side of the driver's face. For an instant he felt the fear stab at him again; was this driver another of the spies that seemed to permeate every nook and cranny of this city? And, if so, which side held his loyalty? He pressed back into the corner of the back seat and dropped his hand onto the arm rest, his hand near the door handle – just in case.

His mind continued to race with images of the patrol and the cold punch of fear in his stomach as he considered what could have happened if he had been caught on the wrong side of the wall. He tried to force himself to calm down; he told himself that the danger was passed and that he was safe. Safe, he thought, for the moment. Berlin was a hotbed of activity. There were more soldiers, police, spies and free agents playing all of the angles in one city block of the city than in most countries. Anyone could be anyone and everyone was probably somebody else entirely.

For a moment he considered that this might be the one city on the planet where he truly belonged. He and his alter-ego Jud Carson could get along nicely in a city where everyone was someone else, too. But the reality that he was playing out of his own backyard and far out of his league was not lost. He had been lucky before; he was going to have to be a damned sight more than that this time.

Berlin wasn't a place where reputations were lost. In his brief time since he arrived he had already realized that this was a place where people were lost – and never heard of again.

The taxi stopped for a traffic light and he turned his attention to the movie theater on the other side of the glass. A poster for the feature decorated the length of the wall beside the entrance. A nude woman holding a cocktail glass smiled at him from the advertisement. Well, he thought, that's something you don't see in Benton, Pennsylvania.

He considered if the Germans lack of outrage over full-frontal nudity in advertising was because they were compensating for the sins of their history or the love of life that was accentuated by the desperation of the threats that surrounded them daily. Knowing that you might be at ground zero of the next and final war could certainly change a person's perspective on what was morally acceptable.

For Berliners the war that had shattered their country had never really ended in many ways. The heady days of the quick victories at the beginning of the Second World War had turned into the nightmare of defeat followed by the Soviet blockade and decades of the Cold War with its unrelenting, grinding tension.

*****

Paula moved to the other side of the room and kicked off her shoes then busied herself freeing her blouse from where it was tucked into her skirt.

"And you think that you can find the gun that

was actually used?" She slid the zipper of her skirt down but left the hook and eye at the waistband secured. She turned her attention to the row of buttons on her blouse, deftly flicking the white plastic discs free and letting the silk cascade away from her body.

Jerome turned back to her just as she let the blouse slip from her shoulders. She caught the collar between the thumb and index finger of her left hand and tossed it toward the armchair in the corner where it draped over the chair's back. She didn't seem to consider his presence as she slipped the hook from her skirt and, with a wiggle of her hips, let it fall and pool around her ankles.

"Ye – yes," he managed, struggling to turn back toward the window and let the lights of the Berlin night drive the image of the woman behind him from his mind. Too late he realized that her reflection floated above him in the bedroom window. Behind him Paula continued to undress. She unclasped the garters to her stockings – who still wore garters and stockings? he asked himself – and rolled the nylons down her firm thighs and calves before sitting on the edge of the bed and removing them the rest of the way. She rose and took the two steps to the armchair, dropped the stockings over the skirt that lay on the arm and pulled the garter belt around so that she could see to undo the hook that held it closed. She let it dangle from her hand for an instant, glanced toward Jerome and then dropped it on the seat of the armchair.

"There aren't that many possibilities," he went on at last. "Whoever it was, it had to be someone in that house that night. They had to know that you had a gun and they had to know where to find it."

"Are you sure about that?" Paula asked. "It isn't like I'm a pistol-packin' momma who always knows where her shootin' iron is." She turned to face the window and threaded first her right then left arms through the straps of her bra, leaving the cups covering her breasts. "After all, anyone who had access to that room could have made the switch," she said. She continued to stand and stare at Jerome's back as he tried to ignore her.

He shook his head. "That may be true, but the most important part wasn't switching the barrels. It was switching them back. And that had to happen that night and it had to happen after the shooting but before the cops showed up and froze the scene." His eyes flicked up and met hers. "What the hell are you doing?" he asked at last.

"I'm getting ready for bed," she said with a slight smile. "I was hoping that you could give me a hand. Or something."

He sighed and turned around. "I kinda got that message," he said.

Paula let the cups of her bra fall away to reveal full, slightly up-turned breasts capped with rosy areolas and puffy, thick nipples of a slightly darker shade. She turned the bra around as she had the garter, undid the hooks and tossed it onto the armchair. This time, however, he thought he noticed a tremble in her hands. The bra barely touched the edge of the chair seat, seemed to teeter, then slid down onto the carpet. He turned his gaze back to the nearly-nude woman before him.

"Is this a game?"

Paula brushed her hands lightly over her

nipples and the slightly inverted buds sprung out in full bloom. She pressed her lips together and shook her head slightly. "This, Jud," she said, hooking her thumbs inside the material of the light blue panties, "is me telling you that I want to spend the night with you."

"And the reason is?"

"There are a lot of them," she said. "First, I find you very attractive. Second, I appreciate what you are going through for me. Third," she began to push the panties down, "I may be going to prison for a very long time and I don't think that I will be dating much there. At least not on my terms. And there is the strong possibility that if I am sentenced my own country will make sure that I don't make it to prison. In a permanent way." The panties lay at her feet and she put her hands on her hips. "And, damn it, I like sex, Jud, and I would like to see if you like it with me."

He let his gaze drink her in slowly. His desire for her was undeniable. Still, he stood with his back to the window.

"I come by this honestly," she said softly. "I am a barley-child."

"This isn't the way that I do business," Jerome said softly.

"You want me," Paula said just as softly.

"Yeah, I guess that'd be pretty obvious even in the dark," Jerome conceded. "I think there are some East Germans who could testify to that."

Paula ignored the quips. "And I need to be wanted right now," she went on. Paula lowered her hands from her hips and her left knee bent slightly to the right, partially obscuring the object of his recent attention. "I could really use a good cry," she said.

He stepped to the right, moving toward the

bathroom. There he took the robe from its hanger and returned. As he approached her Paula let her head dip. He draped the robe over her shoulders and tilted her chin up. "You have no idea how much I wish I could," he said. "And, maybe, when this thing is all over, maybe you'll consider making the offer again."

Paula smiled wanly. "You know that I won't do that," she said. "A girl has to have some pride."

He touched her cheek gently and stepped back. "If this is – done – " he said, "I'd like to get back to work."

Paula slipped her arms through the sleeves of the robe and nodded. "Let's have a seat, order some coffee and see what we have." She picked up the telephone and pressed buttons, waited, then spoke a few words in German. When she had replaced the receiver she opened the drawer in the nightstand and took out a notebook and pen.

Jerome was already seated at the small table on the other side of the room when she joined him.

"I think we need to put a list together of everyone who was in that house that night," he said.

Paula plopped down unceremoniously across from him, the bubble of her allure had been punctured and she was no longer the femme fatale she had been a moment ago. "This would be easier with a little relief to work out the tension," she said. Now she was a skilled intelligence analyst with a sergeant's sense of priorities and proprieties.

Jerome smiled, realizing that the crisis had passed. "Let's worry about saving your ass first," he said. "Then you can think about what to do with it."

"The police already have this list," Paula said.

"And they are pretty certain that they already

have their perpetrator. This may be the Federal Republic of Germany rather than California, but cops is cops. When they figure they have the bad guy they quit looking for the bad guy."

Paula shrugged but nodded. "There was Florian's wife," she said. "But I think we can rule her out."

"Really? Why so sure?"

"A bunch of reasons. Age – interests – inclinations. Take your pick."

"Do tell, Marzipan."

Paula squinted and looked up at him. "'Marzipan'?"

The corner of Jerome's mouth twitched.

Paula shook her head and snorted. "I've been called a lot of things," she mused.

"I believe you."

"Hey!"

"You were saying?"

"Florian's wife is too old to care. She got all of the respect and cow-towing that her position demanded and that was enough. She had had her share of affairs when she was younger and Florian had always been a gent about that, too. It was their arrangement and it worked out fine."

"Okay. Who else was there?"

"The household staff. Three of them – a maid, a cook, and the butler. Before you say anything: The butler didn't do it. Neither did the other two."

"I tend to agree, but I reserve the right to come back to this."

"Agreed."

"That doesn't leave us much," he sighed.

"Sorry," Paula pushed her chair back from the

table and stretched her legs. The robe fell away from her legs as she did so and he gave into the temptation of admiring them. He knew that she was watching him but she did not make a point of it. Neither did he. The moment had passed and the tension was gone.

'I'm not," he said at last.

"And that's because?"

"That means that we know who did it."

"Really? Florian's nephew Berrin was the only other person in the house that night. Unless, you mean that there could be someone we didn't know about."

"I can't know about someone that I don't know about," he said.

"Well, that means," Paula started, then turned her attention to the light rap at the door. She rose, crossed to it and held it open for the middle-aged woman who entered with the coffee service. When the tray was on the table between them Paula said something in German to the woman who smiled and replied "Gern geschehen" with a wave of her hand.

When the door was closed again Paula turned back to the table where Jerome was pouring from the silver pot into porcelain cups.

"Look," she began again. "I would love to come up with a culprit, but Berrin didn't have a motive. He didn't care one way or another about me, or me and his uncle, and he was already in the will. So long as his aunt is alive he couldn't inherit more. So, no motive. And the only reason he was there that night was because his aunt asked him to driver her."

Jerome studied her over the rim of his cup. "Wrong," he said simply. "Florian was killed by someone in that house that night. If it wasn't his wife or the servants it was you or his nephew. It wasn't you. It was the nephew."

Paula held her silence for a moment. She considered his words then took a sip of the coffee. She put the cup down and tapped the edge of the saucer with a manicured, crimson nail. "So, now what?" she asked. "Like you said, the cops have done all of the investigation that they need to. I'm the patsy."

"We do the same thing I said the first night we met," Jerome replied. "We prove it."

Jerome sipped from his cup. "I'm going to have a list of questions," he said. "Assuming that you still have friends in the city."

"A few," Paula acknowledged. "Just what kind of questions?"

"The kind that it would take friends like yours to answer." He glanced at his watch, stood and stretched.

"Don't count on them being there for me," she said softly. "They can't afford it."

"Well, then, we'll just have to make it affordable," Jerome said.

Paula studied her cup as he stepped past her and went to the door. "I'll see you later," he said, twisting the handle and stepping into the hallway. "You should probably lock this."

"Depends on who is going to come calling," Paula answered. He stepped out and closed the door quietly. He could hear the tumblers fall into place as he waited.

*****

Notebook 24, Entry 22

"I made calls to some of the other hires in town and conveyed the badge's condolences and concerns then cooled my heels at the *Bourbon and Branch* until the waiters started putting chairs on empty tables. They were giving me and the other die-hards quiet, pointed looks so I paid my tab and headed for the door.

"Being stood up by a client wasn't something that I had never been through before but this time I had let myself look forward to smelling the faint jasmine of her perfume and to hearing the mix of accents that labeled her speech like stickers on a steamer trunk. When she didn't appear I felt like a kid who got to the theater too late to see the feature and was left with the memories of the previews from last week. I stepped out onto the sidewalk, set my cup of Stan's chili on the parking valet's table long enough to tie the belt of my trench coat around me and stand my collar up against the damp.

"Cab, mister?"

"I looked back at the source of the question. He was twenty. Maybe. Thin and seemed thinner in the black vest and dimmed lights. His pale face seemed to float in the air.

"I shook my head. "I'm going to do some walking," I said.

"It was a San Francisco night like any other, but maybe a little more so. The fog seemed to be heavier and it swallowed sound and light more quickly – a hungry grey ghost that haunted the city and wouldn't let it ever forget the things that had gone on in the death shroud that never left its shoulders. I made my way to the corner of Jones and

O'Farrell and looked back at the now-closed *Bourbon and Branch*. The lights were out and it was as if the place didn't even exist anymore. I made my way down to the corner of Bush and Van Ness, between Japantown and Lower Nob Hill.

"There was no particular reason to go there at two in the morning. No bars. No one to talk to. Just a used car dealership, a coffee shop, and a deli that would be serving breakfast in a few hours. I had found myself walking those blocks a lot over the last few years. It was quiet and no one there knew me. I could walk and think and not worry that someone was going to try to even a score with me while I wasn't paying attention.

"I wasn't sure what to make of Elaine Merriman or of Jeffrey Brighton. Nothing seemed to add up in this screwy case. If Brighton didn't have the letter why did she insist that he did? If he did, why was he willing to pay me to get it from someone else? I was busily not paying attention when I turned up an alley and realized a moment later that I was going to have to turn around or learn how to climb a concrete wall without a ladder.

\-   *When the Clock Strikes Dead*
Jud Carson, P.I.

*****

"Can I buy you a drink?" Jerome asked.

Daisy looked up at him without raising her head and smiled. "I don't know if I should drink with you," she said. Still, her left hand moved toward the bar sink's drying rack and she chose a short tumbler.

"Bad policy to drink with the customers?"

Daisy shook her head slightly. "I'm just careful *which* customers I drink with," she answered. "And what it is that I drink when I do."

"Whiskey?" Jerome offered.

"I might have a problem with my words if I drink whiskey with you," she said. She dropped a coaster from the stack then placed the glass on it between them. "I have a feeling that it would affect my words."

"I know that problem," Jerome said. "It can make me slur my S's."

Daisy shook her head again and poured herself a double Tullamore Dew. "That's not what I mean," she said. She raised her glass and waited until he had done the same.

"What I mean," she said, tipping her glass to touch his, "is that drinking whiskey with you will make me more likely to say 'Yes'."

Chapter Eleven

Daisy was still sleeping as Jerome tried to decipher the German way of making coffee. After searching cupboards and cabinets he had finally managed to locate the coffee and the pot. Filters were still eluding him. He was about to give up in favor of leaving the small apartment above Finnegan's to look for an open café when he realized that she was standing in the kitchen doorway watching him.

"Are all Californians so helpless?" she asked. She was wearing his shirt, unbuttoned, and a smile. He noted that he liked the shirt on her much more than on him, but preferred it on the floor to either.

"Well," he said, moving over to her and leaning in for a kiss, "we're good at some things."

Daisy laughed and covered her mouth. "No!" she giggled, "I have not brushed my teeth!"

"That much I managed to do," he said, moving his head back and forth as he sought an opportunity to kiss her.

"How is that? Did you bring a toothbrush?" she laughed and continued to avoid him.

"Nope, I brought a finger!" He pulled her to him. "Now come here, woman!"

She sighed as though she were a helpless damsel and seemed to collapse in his arms. He kissed her gently at first, then, as she began to respond, her embarrassment forgotten for the moment, more passionately. Her resolve returned a moment later, however and she pressed her hands against his shoulders. He moved away with a last press of his lips on her cheek. "Good morning," he said.

"Guten Morgan," she replied. She turned her head and looked at him from the side with a warm smile. "Go and shower," she said. "I will make the coffee like a good frau."

"Can I make a call first?"

She nodded to the phone on the wall then busied herself with the coffee.

A moment later Jerome had retrieved the phone number from his shirt pocket, a task that produced a new flurry of giggles from Daisy, and dialed the number.

"Dare? Jud. Time to wake up and put on your business face."

"Where the hell are you?" Colfield asked.

"A gentleman never tells," Jerome answered, drawing a sly smile and wink from Daisy as she moved past him. "I'll give you all the details later. Right now I need you to put your contacts and money to work."

"I can't say how good the contacts are right now. A lot of people are not looking to be known as my best buddy. But the money is still spendable. What is it that I am supposed to spend my wife's inheritance on now?"

"Paula's boyfriend has a nephew named Berrin. I think he's a Schumann, too. I need to know what can be known about him. Can you make that happen?"

"I don't know how long it's going to take," Colfield said.

"And I don't know how long we have left,"

Jerome answered.

"Are you on your way here?"

The coffee had begun to perk and Jerome glanced through the open kitchen doorway. He could see into the bedroom where Daisy stood looking at him with a slight smile. Satisfied that she had his attention she slowly reached up with both hands and pushed his shirt from her shoulders, letting it fall to the floor at her feet.

"Uhm," Jerome said, "it's going to be a while." He hung up the phone without turning.

*****

"That's the same shirt that you had on last night," Colfield said.

"Yes, but it is a whole new smile on my face," Jerome returned. "Did you manage to get any dirt on this guy?"

"Berrin Schumann? There isn't any."

"Has to be," Jerome insisted.

"Why is that?"

"Because he is a murderer. Murderers are always dirty. I read that in a book. Or maybe I'll write that in a book."

"Well, maybe he isn't a murderer, then. Look, he's a salesman for a book publisher – "

"I told you he was dirty."

Colfield sighed.

"Go ahead, don't mind me," Jerome urged.

"He had been living in Kaiserslautern out in the zone until a year ago."

"Hold on, Dare. Do you want to translate that for me?"

"K-Town, Kaiserslautern, it's the biggest American enclave outside of the States."

"Why?"

"That's simple: Ramstein Air Force Base, Kindsbach Cave, all of the kasernes. They are all American military bases. The zone is anyplace in Germany that's outside of Berlin and the East."

"Okay, got it – go to it. Why is he living in Little America?"

"Mostly because he was selling books to Americans, from what I can gather."

Jerome seemed to be considering Dare's information for a moment. Then, "Doesn't that seem a little weird?"

"What?"

"The fact that a German wants to sell books to Americans."

"Germany had the first ever and still has the biggest book fairs. Americans have more money. No, it doesn't seem weird, Jud – we're in their country, but most of Germany isn't occupied territory. Only Berlin."

"Okay. So then he moves to Berlin."

"Yeah, he got transferred. Which worked out because his uncle had to move from Bonn to here about the same time."

"I thought that he had a mansion here."

"Estate. Yeah, he had that, but he lived most of the time in Bonn because it's the capital. He got moved here to work on some special project."

"And met Paula."

Colfield nodded. "He needed a good liaison with the American intel community. She was perfect for the job."

"So why did you say this "'Worked out'?"

"His uncle was old. He could run errands for him, things like that."

Jerome frowned. "His uncle was rich and a government official. One that needed a hot American woman to run interference with the international intelligence community. He didn't need a relative to run errands for him."

"Whiskey Tango Foxtrot, Oscar," Colfield said softly.

"Does that mean what I think it means?" Jerome asked.

Colfield nodded. "And then some. It means that the nephew is dirty." He reached into the briefcase beside the table and pulled out a file. "Here's everything that I could get on him for the last two months."

Jerome opened the file and skimmed it. A moment later he closed it again and drummed his fingers on the polished table top. "I'm going to have to go to London tonight," he said.

"I'll get you a car."

"I think that I would rather fly."

Colfield shook his head. "To get you to the airport, I mean."

Jerome smiled. "Yeah, I know," he said.

*****

Heathrow Airport was the closest thing that Jerome had experienced to home since arriving in Europe. The noise, crowds, and seemingly random lay-out made him finally fight his way to an empty terminal chair and analyze the traffic flow before trying again.

A half hour later he had managed to escape into the night via a taxi that took him to a hotel not far from the downtown area. Once he had settled into his room he switched on the television, clicked through British sitcoms and a talent show until he found the news and kicked off his shoes. He was loosening his tie when the broadcast ended and another British sitcom began. He turned off the set and found the radio beside the bed, dialing in the world service on BBC.

Most of the reports from Bush House were from the Eastern Bloc. Dissidents were continuing to press for reform with their banners raised high and some hard-liners were expected to press back with their rifles leveled. A panel of commentators began to recap the events that had developed over the continent since the beginning of the year. Jerome considered calling Daisy but resisted. She would be at work and didn't need him acting like a school boy while she concentrated on earning a living. He was not her first dance, he reminded himself. She was a grown woman who was not about to be waiting for him to call and wondering why he hadn't.

He took a long bath before placing the call to Finnegan's. She had been wondering how long it would take him, she said.

*****

Notebook 24, Entry 23

"I turned back just in time to see them step out of the fog and shadows.

"Sure, it takes the equivalent of an idiot rookie on

the stupid side of slow and probably half-drunk thrown in to let himself get cornered in a dead-end street with nothing but a ten-foot concrete block wall boxing him in at one end and a trio of more-than-capable broken-nose types at the other. Being un-armed put the cherry on.

"Okay, so that's what it takes. But I don't like calling myself things like that. I wouldn't be surprised if Lt. Martinelli called me that and maybe worse the next time that he saw me. I told myself that I wouldn't care so much then. Dead men don't care about things like that. As far as I could tell, dead men don't care too much about most things.

"I thought about what it was that I still cared about – just what was the tote on the score card that kept me from being in the 'might as well be dead anyway' column of the big book. Not much. A cheap apartment that I was never in. An office that I was rarely in. A trench coat that I could call home. The rest, well…

"So maybe this was it – the night that I let myself in for the last slumber. Maybe I had planned it or let it happen without wanting to admit it. The head-shrinkers could have a field day with it. 'Private-Eye Probably Promoted Own Passing'. Suicide by hood.

"But then – okay – I like Stan's chili. I curled my lips back over my teeth and popped the top off the cardboard container I had picked up at the stand of the closest thing to a friend I had.

"Stan would understand. Well, in fact, he wouldn't care. "Dinner's on you, pal," I snapped. A cloud of spicy steam jetted up just before I tossed the contents into the nearest thug's kisser. He didn't scream. He didn't run away. He was a professional. And he was, for a few seconds, blind. He didn't see the knuckle-duster come out of my pocket and jab at the lantern he called a jaw. He probably didn't even realize that his lights had been put out as he dropped like a pole-axed cow, first to his knees, then, like a slow-motion movie of a redwood coming down, face first onto the rain-slicked asphalt.

"I had my mit in his pocket faster than an IRS agent at a tax-amnesty party. The snub-nosed .38 seemed to jump into my hand like an ex-lover who had come to her senses. The curved, smooth walnut grip nestled into my palm for a snuggle and the hammer offered itself up to be stroked. As I brought it up I could smell the gun-oil. Slightly sweet and slightly metallic. It was a good mix of business and pleasure perfumes that meant both serious, sweaty work and a promise that we'd still be together in the morning if I held up my end of the deal.

"The sleeper's partner in the too-tight tweed had closed the distance, his gat was clear of his jacket and the barrel was coming up in a most un-friendly manner toward my favorite fedora. Before he could finish the thought I had pointed and squeezed just like my old drill instructor had taught me and the Smith and Wesson sang my favorite tune.

"The gout of blood exploded back at me from where the bullet ripped into his knee. A dark red halo sprayed out for an instant and colored the dim black and white. I breathed in the plume of cordite and gunpowder and it coursed through me like the smell of beer stoking the thirst of a factory worker after a long shift.

"This guy wasn't above a scream. The gun dropped from his hand and clattered to the street as his priorities were shifted by the sudden introduction of agony. By the time that he had hit the high notes he had dropped to my level where I was still crouched. I grabbed him by the lapels and twisted him until his beefy back was between me and the remaining bruiser: the one with the narrow face and darting eyes. The one with the .45 in his hand. His first shot went wild and I took a spray of crimson from the sleeper's body. At least he hadn't been awake when he had died.

"His next round would have ended my night permanently if it hadn't been for my tweed covered shield. The heavy, slow slug punched into his back and he began to scream and jerk. I had my hands full just trying to keep him between me and certain death.

"The .45 barked twice more and the screams went silent like a Philco when you pull the plug. The automatic's barrel spit orange-yellow tongues of fire like a Chinese dragon and I could feel the heat from the burning gases as the shooter continued to rush forward, his long, thin finger still jerking the trigger. He was close enough now that I could see the slide jack back and the spent casings leap out of the side port to clatter onto the street like a killer's castanets. The thuds that slammed into my press-ganged protector made him jolt and stiffen. The bullets sent to me had found a different home and I was no longer holding a man by the lapels – I was holding onto a corpse.

"He had gone from being a useful bone-breaker for his boss Jeffrey Brighton to being a high velocity ballistics intercept specialist for me – from bad guy to bullet catcher in one not-so-easy lesson. From somebody's something to a sandbag.

"The shooter didn't seem to be fazed by the turn of events, but now that it was down to just the two of us we were both settling into the dance. I could see his chin lift slightly as he focused his eyes on mine. He could see his only good target: my *cabeza*. And he was going to do it right and right now.

"My right arm came up under my shield's limp left while I used my free hand to keep him steadied in front of me. The revolver in my grip just cleared the tweed-covered armpit. My thumb dragged the hammer back to its locked stop.

"The .38 sounded like a pop gun after the thunder of the .45 but it still only took one shot to end the debate about who was going to make it home and who was going to take a ride to a meat locker. I gave him an extra argument anyway.

"The first bullet took him in the center of his chest and he staggered. The second one punched through the left side of his face; the lead drilled through from just below the sharp cheekbone and blew through the rear of the top of his head taking hopes and dreams and brain and bone with it. He crumpled like a dropped accordion and even let out one last, long sigh. His coda was a broken note."

-   *When the Clock Strikes Dead*

*****

"I need to get to a library," Jerome said to the cabbie.

"And what library would that be?" the driver asked. He glanced back at his passenger as he pulled into the traffic.

"I – don't know," Jerome said.

"Well, now, we're going to have a bit of a problem getting there, then," the driver said.

"I don't know London," Jerome offered.

"Never would've dreamed it," the man said. "Suppose you give me an idea of just what we are looking for and maybe we can come up with the right place to get it."

"I need a place that has lots of newspapers," Jerome began.

The cabbie nodded.

"In English," Jerome went on.

"We've got a surprising number that fit the bill so far."

"Where I can sit and go over them."

"And are you looking for something in particular, sir?"

"I don't know. Something – unusual."

The cabbie squinted at him in the rear-view mirror. "Just how 'unusual'?"

"I don't know. What do you mean?"

"Well, are we talking 'Amsterdam' unusual or just run-of-the-mill unusual?"

"We can probably leave Amsterdam to Amsterdam," Jerome said.

"Well, then, you sit back and we'll have you to your destination in no time, sir," the driver said.

"And where will that be?"

"Well, if not the oldest, in my way of thinking, the best in the whole of the United Kingdom: The London Library on St. James Square."

Thirty minutes later he had paid his fare, entered the library and made arrangements to view the major London newspapers from the ninth through the twelfth of September. The news item was small and didn't seem to be significant at all. To Jerome it seemed to fill the page. He made notes and within two hours of awakening was on his way back to Heathrow Airport.

*****

The taxi that took him to Finnegan's was gone by the time that he had come back. Despite the promised tip the cabbie had taken off with another fare and Jerome was left wondering what his next move should be. He was tired, hungry and tired in that order he decided, but rather than go to the estate he had sped here for a quick moment with Daisy. She had offered her apartment key but he knew that he would have to be on the job the first thing in the morning and she would be needing sleep. He had pressed the velvet box that held the cloisonné brooch, a daisy, that he had found in a gift shop at Heathrow, into her hand, and been rewarded with a quick kiss and smile.

He had stepped back when she rushed to him again, grabbing his hand and drawing him into the short hallway that lead into the kitchen behind the darts room. "I haven't anything to give you!" she said with a frown.

"I'll be happy with another kiss," he suggested. She pressed forward and kissed him warmly. Then, breaking away she reached into her back pocket and pulled out a pen. "This is my lucky pen," she said with mock seriousness. "I always get the best tips when I use this pen. I want you to have it." She tucked the silver-barreled instrument into his inside jacket pocket and kissed him again.

A moment later they had emerged from the hallway and he stepped back out into the night.

On foot and unsure of himself he considered his options. He doubted that he would see any taxis rolling in this neighborhood, so, reluctantly, he turned and began making his way toward the UBahn. He would find a cab there. As he neared the busier streets the music of the clubs began to spill out. Suddenly he was being pushed down a short flight of stairs and through the doors of a nightclub, its throbbing speakers driving through his weary mind.

He was still being pushed, though gently, forward and in a moment he found himself near another door. Smiling at his luck he pressed the handle down and stepped through. Then he noticed that he was not alone in his escape.

"You perhaps would have a match?" the man asked. He was shorter than Jerome, coming only to his chest. But he had the look of a welterweight. His small, quick eyes were like chips of flint and his mouth had been scarred; it looked, Jerome thought, as if the man were used to old-fashioned bare knuckles prize fighting. If it were true, he acknowledged, this guy could probably whip anybody in his weight class.

"I don't smoke," Jerome answered, beginning to ease his way past.

"This does not matter," the man replied. "I do not smoke, either. It is a terrible burden to the health."

Jerome paused and smiled at the curious exchange. It flashed through his mind that, had he not been so tired from the travel and hours that he had been putting in, he might have seen that this was a set-up in time. As it was, all he could do was to try to lean back when the smaller man moved in and head-butted him on the chin. The immoveable object behind Jerome turned out to be the shorter man's companion and between them they quickly shuffled him into the alley behind the club.

A bare light bulb shown above the back door. Jerome managed to focus up and down the alley enough to realize that he was alone and it that it was doubtful that they could be seen from the street.

"You ask so many questions," the smaller man said. "You should learn that in Germany it is not so polite to ask so many questions." His hands were small but hard and his knuckles seemed disproportionately large. When his punches landed it was like being struck with a board. "We will help you to learn this lesson," he said between blows. He had training in making each punch count. He controlled his breathing and rotated his hips to drive his diamond-hard fists into Jerome's midsection.

After a half-dozen body blows he tilted Jerome's head back with his right hand and began to work on his face with the left. The bruises raised quickly and Jerome could sense that he was about to throw up. With luck he might pass out soon. But, no, the man who stood before him was skilled. Most probably he was a professional. He would not allow Jerome that gentle escape.

"Perhaps you would like to return to your own country and leave Germany to Germans?" He went back to work on Jerome's body again. "And perhaps you will forget the name of Herr Berrin Schumann." He took two quick jabs at Jerome's face and the blood began to flow from the opened wounds. "I think that this would be a very good thing for you to do."

"What makes you think – " Jerome struggled to get his breath before going on, "that I have any interest in this guy?"

The short man smirked. "Information," he said, "it is like a lake, yes? It is everywhere. But when it is being sought out, then there are, what you call, uh, ripples. You have made ripples."

"Waves," Jerome corrected. "You mean I've been making waves."

"Yes, good, thank you," the small man said. "You have done me a good thing with my English." He spun Jerome around until he faced the big man who grabbed him in a bear hug. The small man went to work on Jerome's kidneys with his fists.

"Now we do you a good thing. We teach," he grunted as he punched, "you," grunt, "to not be," grunt, "so curious."

The man in front of Jerome began to tighten his embrace and Jerome struggled to draw his breath. In a moment the lights had stopped spinning in front of Jerome's closed eyes. They had turned black.

*****

"Jerome!" Strong hands shook him gently.

"What do you think, Doc?"

Jerome opened his eyes, or, rather his left eye, grimaced at the white light that seared into his pain-wracked brain and shut it quickly. When he squeezed his eyes shut against the intruding light his right eye began to throb and he could feel a wetness begin to trickle from it across his cheek.

Doc – he presumed it was Doc – cursed softly. "He's bleeding again, Sarge. We ought to get him to a hospital. Or down to the infirmary at least."

"Patch him up. He can't afford to go to a hospital. And if they get him into the infirmary we won't see him again."

Doc was working on him. He felt gentle hands cleaning, pressing, and bandaging. "I don't know, Sarge. He could lose the damned thing if he doesn't get some real care."

"He will, he will," Sarge soothed. Jerome could imagine Sarge putting his hands on Doc's upper arms, just below the shoulders and squeezing gently like a coach encouraging a star quarterback. You just get in there and call the play and we are going to win this thing yet, the coach would say.

"You just get him stable and we're going to get him the best medical care in this city," Sarge said. "But we don't need to run him through the Berlin Brigade or Daddy Doyle Larson's operations. We'll get him a hotshot German doctor mit der Grosse resume."

"Jerome," Sarge said again. "Are you in there? Your pal Dare Colfield is on his way to get you."

"How'd you – " Jerome felt a fresh fear wash over him as he realized that the whispered, hoarse sounds had come from his own lips. " – get me?"

"Almost didn't," Sarge said. There was almost an apology in his tone. "We lost you for a few minutes in that club you ducked into. By the time we tracked you down you were all alone and not up to dancing."

Jerome waited for Sarge to say that he was sorry. Sarge didn't say it. Instead he whistled softly and whispered, "Sierra Hotel."

"Yeah," Doc agreed. "and this guy had a helluvalota 'Sierra Hotel' to him."

"Where am I?" Jerome managed. Another part of his mind was trying to figure out what 'Sierra Hotel' meant but he wasn't too concerned.

"TCA," Doc answered.

Jerome waived a hand. "Too much," he mumbled.

"Templehof Central Airport," Sarge explained. "This is the big enchilada in Berlin. Ran the airlift right into here not that long ago. Now it's a lot of things. Mostly its Grade A U.S. Air Force."

"Spies," Jerome said.

"Naw – bunch of damned admin clerks. And Doc, here. Takes care of our paper cuts."

"My name," Jerome managed. "How'd you know my name?"

"You must have told us," Sarge said.

"You're lying," Jerome said. "And not well – so you want me to know."

"He's got to shut up or he's just going to keep bleeding," Doc said softly.

"Okay," Sarge said. Jerome wasn't sure but he thought that the man was speaking to both him and Doc at once. "Look, we managed to find out a little bit about you," Sarge said. "Like your real name. And your birthday. And your favorite color and the name of the first girl you kissed. And the last one, too."

Jerome tried to open his eyes and sit up but someone held him back with little effort and a hand was placed gently over his eyes. "Relax," Doc said. "Keep 'em closed."

"Don't worry," Sarge said. "We're the good guys. She's safe. We've been watching you since you got into town."

"Can you tell me who those guys were?"

"Hell – don't you know? Those boys work for the East German Stasi. A nasty bunch of cloak-and-brass knuckle types. I know why you're here – and I know that you snuck across the border – but I don't know why you got jumped tonight. What did they tell you?"

"They didn't like the way I treated the ticket taker," Jerome said. He tried to smile but it was too much effort.

"Sure," Sarge said. "That's probably it. But if you ever come to your senses and want to let me know the real reason you just tell Dare that you want to talk. He knows the room number."

"Don't tell him," Jerome said.

"Don't tell him what? That you got the hell kicked out of you by some Stasi thugs? I think he can two-oh-two the hell out of that one."

"'Two-oh-two'?" Jerome's head ached and he knew that he should let it go but couldn't.

"It means to figure something out. Air Force lingo."

"Spies," Jerome said again.

"Have it your way. You paid for the ride tonight. You can call us dog catchers for all I care."

"Don't tell Dare who I am," Jerome said,

managing to get back to his original thought.

"Oh, the whole 'Jud Carson' thing, sure, no problem," Sarge assured him. "But I can't say that he doesn't already know. He used to be on the bright side when he was working here."

"As an admin clerk," Jerome chided.

"That's right," Sarge agreed. "As an admin clerk."

Jerome felt himself drifting into the shadows of sleep but Doc and Sarge kept bringing him back each time. At last there was a muffled knock and he knew that his friend had arrived.

"We have to stop meeting like this," Dare said, kneeling down.

"Dare – I think I'm about to wrap this thing up," Jerome said thickly.

"You bet," Dare said. His voice was soothing and his words meant to assure rather than agree.

"No, really," Jerome said. He managed to grab Colfield's coat by the lapels and, though he could not open his eyes, he thrust his face close to the lawyer's. "I know I'm close. Really close."

"What makes you think so?" Dare asked.

"'Cause they just beat me half to death. They don't ever do that for nothing – remember?"

"You bet," Colfield said. He turned his head away from Jerome's. "Guys – do we have a wheelchair or something?"

"Got an office chair. It's got wheels." Jerome could hear the chair being moved toward him. A moment later he was lifted by two men and put on the worn leather seat. Belts secured him to the seat and back and he was draped with a blanket for the ride down the hall and into the elevator. With his eyes closed he imagined the elevator of *The Colonnades* with Gwendolyn waiting for him in the compartment. When she smiled at him her eyes became small pieces of flint. He felt that he was going to retch but there was nothing in his stomach and the feeling passed.

"Dare," Jerome said as the doors closed and the elevator began its descent.

Colfield leaned close.

"I'm going to need a doctor."

The lawyer patted his shoulder gently

"Tough son of a bitch," Sarge said. "He took one hell of a beating tonight."

"Sierra Hotel," Colfield said. "You only know the half of it."

Chapter Twelve

It was two days before Jerome could sit up for more than an hour at a time and three before he could get around his room at the estate without help. Now, four days after what he thought of as his private conference with foreign intelligence officers, he had made his way downstairs for the first time and taken his place at the breakfast table with Claire at the table's waist and Dare Colfield opposite him at the other end.

"Jesus, Jud, I think that we may be way out of our league here," Dare said as he poured himself a second cup of coffee. "I think we have to accept that it's time to take care of your account and let you get back to California before something else happens to you." The mid-morning light was streaming in through the French doors that led to the gardens below. Though the chill of the season prevented having the doors open, the view was still nearly story-book. Claire set her cup on its saucer and sat back, resting her elbows lightly on the chair's delicately carved arms. She said nothing but glanced from her husband to her friend Jud Carson and back again.

Jerome sighed, stretched his neck slowly from side to side and scratched absently at the bristle of his un-shaved chin, taking care to avoid the bruises and bandaged cuts. Most of the puffiness was gone from his left eye and mouth. "Quittin' time, huh?" He let his right hand drop to the table top with a slight thud. "Oh, that's right, you're the boss here, right?

You gets to say when it's quittin' time."

"Cute," the lawyer said. Although there was a slight edge to his voice it was clear that he would not rise to the bait that his friend had used to chum the conversation. "I've seen *Gone With the Wind*, too. But this aint Tara. Hell, it isn't even Pennsylvania!" He pushed his chair back and seemed to be about to stand but instead put his hands on his knees and sighed. "We don't have the assets here," he went on at last. "I think that I may be able to work something out with the Germans. Maybe get Paula back to the States. But we don't want to have any run-ins with the local law or it could all get very testy very quickly."

"You don't quite mean get her back to the States." Claire said. "You mean that you might be able to arrange for Paula to serve her time in America, don't you?"

Dare pressed his lips together and nodded once. "At least she could be closer to family and support," he said. "Maybe later – "

"I could get commissary privileges?" Paula asked from the doorway.

"It's not like that!" Dare protested.

"It's exactly like that," Jerome shot back. "We haven't been able to beat this thing yet and you're ready to cut a deal."

"Were you ready – before – when I was – " Claire stopped, unable to finish the question for fear of its impact on her husband.

Dare's head shot up and his eyes locked onto hers.

"Not for an instant," Jerome said. "The idea of giving up never crossed his mind. He was going to get you out of that mess no matter what or how long it took."

"Lucky girl," Paula said from her post in the doorway. "Wish I had a knight on a charger like that. How much does it cost?"

"Cheap shot, Paula," Dare said.

"Yeah, well, I'm a cheap date, remember?" She crossed to the other side of the room and stood looking out onto the gardens. "I'm going to miss this," she said simply. "I hope they have real grass on the rec yard. My luck I'll be restricted to a xystus." She turned back to the three of them. "That's an indoor rec area." She shook her head and her voice waivered slightly. "Don't know why I know that. If it's all the same to you, I'd rather spend my next decade or two here in Germany. They'll deport me afterward."

"Paula," Dare began, his eyes still on Claire's, "you know that the intelligence community isn't going to want you to end up in a foreign prison – even one in a friendly country."

"Then they ought to do something about it!" Claire said.

"They will – but it won't be something that any of us like," Jerome put in.

"I'm well aware of that," Paula said. "But come on, Dare, as long as you've known me! Do you really think that I am going to go quietly into that good cell block?"

"For God's sake, Paula! We're talking about your life!"

"Yeah," Paula said with a trace of a laugh. "That's what we're talking about – *my* life." She seemed about to cry but managed to hold back the tears. "See," she said, managing her slightly crooked smile, "I haven't been really scared until now. I knew that I didn't do this thing. And I knew that I had friends – well *a* friend – who believed in me. And *he* had friends who believed in him. So," she took a deep breath and squared her shoulders. "So, I thought 'I'll get through this.' But now, well," she shook her head and grimaced. "Now that I see how this is going to play out, well, I'd rather you just deal me out. I'll call the prosecutor's office and tell them that I am not going to have a defense. I'll turn myself in and get this over with."

"They will kill you," Dare said.

"The Germans?" Claire asked.

"The Americans," Jerome answered. "There's a lot of secret stuff in her noggin. They wouldn't want her to spend years in a German prison figuring out how to trade it for a slice of freedom."

"You love her that much," Claire said softly.

Dare turned to look at her again. "I can't take chances with her life."

"You'd rather see her safe in prison in America than – " she glanced at Paula.

"It's okay, Claire," Paula said. "You can use the word. Dead. But the fact is that I'd rather be dead than in prison."

Jerome shoved his chair back. "Okay. I've had enough. We aren't going to settle for either one of those alternatives. We've hit the ice and lost traction for a little bit. But we're back on the road."

"And just what the hell does that mean?" the lawyer asked.

"It means, dear boy, that I have solved this case. Nobody is going to prison – or die. At least no one that is present here."

"And just how did this come about?" Claire

asked.

"Brilliant detective work," Jerome answered expansively. "Great contacts in the shadow world of intrigue and espionage. And the massaging of information sources with ample amounts of your greenbacks."

"What in the hell are you talking about?" Dare asked.

"I know who did the deed."

"You *think* you know," Paula corrected. She approached the table and took a seat across from Claire who reached out to take Paula's hand in both of hers.

Dare rose and poured coffee for the other three while Jerome stretched back and rested the back of his head in his cupped hands. He smiled and shook his head to continue while his friend moved around the table. When Colfield was seated again Jerome took a deep breath and blew it out forcefully. With it he seemed to dispel the last vestige of the cloud that had darkened the room. The lawyer's argument had faded like a bad dream and none of them would ever consider it again. He doubted if it would ever be discussed even in the distant future.

"No, I *know*," he said. "And I think I even know why."

"But can you prove it?" Colfield asked.

"Of course not!" Jerome laughed then winced at the effort. "But that doesn't mean that I won't be able to – that's what I am supposed to be good at!"

*****

"Don't you guys ever drink?" Paula stood and

stretched. Despite their best efforts both Jerome and Colfield found themselves watching and admiring the display. Paula twisted her hips and shook off some of the ache of having sat too long. "Down, boys, you're both on strict diets, remember?"

"Yeah," Colfield said, "sure we drink. We drink all the time."

"That's right," Jerome put in. "How many pots of this stuff have we finished off?" He looked at his empty coffee cup.

"Sad, boys, very sad." Paula leaned against the back of the dining room chair and stretched her back. "I meant a *real* drink. You know – whiskey – bourbon – gin – schnapps. Even beer. A *drink*."

"Well," Jerome began, "we don't really feel – "

"Yeah, 'cause we don't feel that it would be – you know – "

"That's right," Jerome agreed. "So – it's like – "

"Goes for both of us, right?" Colfield looked at Jerome who nodded firmly.

"You bet."

"Oh, that's *sad*," Paula said, shaking her head. She came around the end of the table and went to the sideboard. Turning two glasses upright she scooped ice from the bucket into each then splashed bourbon over the ice. Satisfied, she turned back to the two men who sat watching her in silence. "Drink up, boys," she said, putting a glass in front of each.

"Well, I'm not, uh," Jerome said, pushing the glass in front of him away.

"Me, neither," Colfield seconded the vote and action.

"Look, guys, I appreciate the gesture. I really do." She went back to her place and sat. "But you drinking or not drinking won't make me drink or keep me from it. Thanks. You're kind and considerate. Now bottoms up."

The two men looked from her to each other, then reached for and drained their glasses.

"Great. A pair of drunks! You two are cut off!"

"Well, maybe Jud is," Claire said as she entered the room. "But Dare owes me!" She leaned over to give Paula a quick hug before going on to stand beside her husband's chair. "What have I missed?"

"That we are sensitive guys on a diet," Jerome answered.

"Aren't you the same one who re-arranged Tommy Greene's priorities?" Claire asked. She had moved to the sideboard, selected a glass and was fixing herself a drink.

"Meaning?"

"Meaning you didn't used to be so sensitive."

Jerome nodded. "Good point," he agreed. "You and Dare need to get out."

Colfield looked at his friend and raised an eyebrow. "Say again – you're coming in garbled and stupid."

"Take your beautiful wife out to dinner, mouth-piece. I've got detective work to do. You're impeding my progress."

"Jud," Claire said, setting her glass aside. "I didn't mean to – "

He waived her off. "No, you're fine; in fact, you're great. But you're also right. I need to get to this thing and I'm not getting it done with so many bodies in the room."

"Am I being sent out, too?" Paula asked.

"Nope. It looks like you and I are going to be spending the night together."

"Grrrowwll," Paula chided. "About time!"

"Uh, no. We are going to be very busy working." Jerome turned to Colfield who had yet to move or respond. "'Night Dare."

"'Night, Jud," the lawyer answered. He rose and joined Claire at the sideboard. "Just like old times," he said, draining her glass. She smiled, shook her head, and followed him out of the room.

When they were alone again Jerome moved closer to Paula. "So," he said.

"So," she repeated.

"Now that we are alone – "

"I'm hungry," she said starting to rise.

He caught her wrist and held it gently but securely. "Talk now, eat later."

Paula looked down at his hand on her wrist and cocked her head toward him. "Are you trying to turn a girl on?" She covered his hand with her free one.

"Why are you doing this?" he asked, releasing his hold. He pushed his chair back and stood, running his hands through his hair and sighing forcefully.

Paula slumped in her chair and clasped her hands in front of her. "I guess you can take the girl out of the intelligence community..."

"But you're not out of it," he countered. "And I get that." He stepped behind her and placed gentle hands on either side of her head. "There are all kinds of secrets in this brain that I don't ever want to know. And I respect the fact that you are keeping your confidences. I really do. But some of them – maybe just one of them – could cost you your life. I'm not willing to take a chance like that. You shouldn't either. I'm old-fashioned enough to think that secrets aren't worth peoples' lives." He began to massage her scalp and neck.

"I'm old-fashioned enough to believe that they are," Paula sighed. She relaxed and let him continue to stroke her, easing the tension away.

"How about this," he asked, "now that we are alone – "

"Nicely done, by the way," Paula interjected.

"Thank you. Now that we are alone, I will ask you questions and you will give me answers and we will figure this thing out together. This is a big break for me – I've never gotten to work with a real spy before."

"Really? How would you know?"

"Touché!" He let his fingers concentrate on the muscles of her neck and the tender spots around her ears. "Do we have a deal?"

"And you'll take my word for it if it's something that I can't talk about?"

"I'm a gentleman," he said.

"I thought you were a detective," she said rolling her neck and letting him ease her tension.

"What was the big thing that Florian was brought here to work on?" he asked.

The muscles of her neck contracted and she sat upright again. "Not something to talk about," she said.

"You're going to have to give me something," he said, beginning to stroke her neck again. He let his hands continue and was soon massaging her shoulders. "I know that he was a spy chief of some sort. I know that he was told to come down here permanently from Bonn. I know that whatever it was he was doing, or going to do, got him killed and you were set up for the fall."

"The whole damned thing is coming down," Paula said. Then, in a rush as though simply slowing down would cut off her words, she pressed on, "Florian had a contact in the Stasi – that's the GDR terrorist police – think Gestapo on steroids – or whatever it is that the Hulk gets juiced up on. His contact was going to start handing over files – a lot of files – in return for being disappeared to a new life."

"I don't get it – isn't that pretty much what spies do?" Jerome asked.

Paula reached up, caught his hands and guided him around to sit beside her. "Not so much. You'd be surprised how little of that goes on. Or how much, depending on how you measure things. But this was huge. If you've missed the news lately let me catch you up: The Iron Curtain is about to come down with a bang. And when it does it's going to fall right on top of a bunch of big-wigs. Well, everybody knows the big-wigs and most of them are going to get away with what they've been up to."

She paused and looked toward the sideboard. "God, I could use a drink," she mused.

Jerome stood up and moved to the other side of the room. "Just water and ice," she said. "And lemon if there is some over there." Then, "But that's not the way it goes for the not-so-big-wigs. The German people will eat them alive."

"And that's where your spy comes in." Jerome put the glass in front of her and sat down again.

Paula nodded. "Yeah, he – or she, for all I know – was going to start handing over files. Those files could – and will – be used to prosecute Stasi agents and informers when this thing is over."

"What happens if the Soviets decide to crack the whip? The Chinese did and everything is back in Marxist-Leninist order."

"Not going to happen. Gorbachev has already sided with the protesters. If he gets through this alive it's all over for the satellite countries. They won't have Papa Bear to back them up anymore."

She took a sip, put the glass down and dipped her finger in, forcing the lemon slice under the water.

"Poor Andelisa," she said absently. "I bet there aren't any famous American detectives working for her."

"Who?"

"Andelisa Kurtz. She was a secretary in our offices."

"Was?"

"She's dead."

"I'm sorry," Jerome said. "Accident?"

Paula shook her head and stirred her lemon slice and ice cubes. "Murdered. Raped and strangled. With her own bra."

Jerome looked up. "When did that happen?"

Paula sighed. "A week – no – just a couple of days before – before Florian was killed."

"Really?" Jerome asked, leaning closer. "Just what did she do in the office?"

Paula made a face. "I don't like to talk about her," she said.

"Why not? Was she a rival?"

"*Hell* no!" Paula snapped. "Oh, she was pretty enough – very pretty. And young. But she wasn't competition for me."

"So why don't you want to talk about her?"

"Because I don't like to talk about people I knew. Who are dead. If I didn't care for them." She lifted her glass again.

"What in the hell are you talking about?" Jerome asked, the exasperation rolling off of his words like steam.

"I thought she wasn't all that bright," Paula said. "Half the time she would just barge into the room like – " She stopped with the glass half way to her lips. He could see it begin to slip from her hand and tumble to the table, ice, lemon, and water splashing everywhere and the glass shattering on impact.

Jerome leaped up and grabbed the back of her chair, hauling her back and away from the broken glass.

Paula turned and looked at him. "Like what?" he asked gently.

"Like she was a spy," Paula said in a small voice.

Jerome stood and held her as she sat quietly for several minutes. Her head rested against his stomach and his arms had gathered her in, his hands cupping her head and he rocked her gently. At last she seemed to draw herself up and, with a nod of her head she moved back. "Well, I certainly have made a mess of this," she said.

He noticed that she was trying to wipe away tears without being too obvious about it. "Here," he said, taking the handkerchief from the breast pocket of his jacket. He turned away toward the French doors that looked out on the night-darkened gardens beyond.

"I could have stopped her, you know," she said.

"That day. But I just played it off. She was always doing something like that."

"I'm not following you," Jerome said. He kept his back to her but he found himself watching the doorway into the room in the reflective glass of the French doors before him. For an instant his memory of Gwendolyn Dean, hipshot and leaning against the door frame behind him, flooded his thinking. But this woman was no Gwendolyn Dean, he thought. He shook off the image.

"We were in the office and she walked in – just a few days before – all of this – *mess* – started. Florian was talking about the Stasi contact. I think she heard him. The next thing you know – she's dead in her apartment and he's dead down the hall from me."

"In her apartment?" Jerome asked.

"Didn't I say that before?"

He shook his head. From his vantage he could see that she had turned and was watching him.

"Do you know anything else about her murder?"

"Sure – she worked for Florian and he had contacts. Let's see, she had had sex, I think I told you that part – "

"No, you said she was raped."

"Well, I guess that I assumed – "

"Can't assume they're the same, Paula. One might be a stranger. The other might be her lover."

"Sorry, I'm not a cop!"

He shook his head and turned back to her. "Hold on! This isn't the same thing as trying to keep the world from going to war or winning for your side if it does. I don't think I would want to try to out think you at your game. Don't beat yourself up because you miss something here."

Paula nodded and, after a deep breath, began again. "Let's see: no sign of forced entry. No prints. She'd had sex. And wine. And she was strangled with her bra. Nobody saw anything. Nobody heard anything. Case open."

"And this happened in the middle of the week?"

Paula nodded. "There was one other thing," she said.

Jerome waited while she sorted it out in her mind. She tapped the fingernails of her right hand against her front teeth as she thought. "There was a receipt from a little boutique. A bra and panty set. Jud, she'd just bought those the same day, or maybe the day before."

"And where were they?"

"She was strangled with the bra. The panties were on the floor next to the bed."

"She was killed by her lover," Jerome said. "You can bet that the cops realize that – what they don't know – and we do – is that Berrin – did I say that right? – was her lover." Jerome sat down beside her again, took her gently by the shoulders and turned her to face him. "Once you tell them that it might help your case."

"Berrin," Paula said. There was a slight inflection that Jerome had not used. "It means 'bear'.

"Bare? Like nude?"

"No, like the animal. It's the symbol of Berlin."

"East or West?"

"Both. And the Soviets."

"That seems about right."

"Paula, you are going to have to get out of here. Tonight."

"Why?"

"Because I know who the killer is – "

"Yeah, you told me – Berrin."

"That's right. But now I know what he is, too."

"And that is?"

"A spy. For the other side. Or maybe both sides. Or maybe just his side. But you can bet that he knows where you are and you can bet he is going to be coming after you."

"Any ideas?"

"How does TCA sound? I think you know somebody called 'Sarge'."

"Jud, I was called 'Sarge'! Half of the U.S. armed forces is called 'Sarge'!"

"This one is in room 207," Jerome said.

"And how do you know that?"

"I tend to pay attention to things when I think it might be the last thing I ever see. Get just what you need and let's get out of here. I don't want to be around when the guys who did this to me show up again."

"I don't think that I've seen you like this before," Paula said.

"That's because it's time to turn the tables for a change."

*****

Notebook 24, Entry 24

"It was noon before the cops cut me loose and I made my way back to my place. I left my clothes where they fell and was down to my skin by the time that I made it to the bathroom and turned on the shower. I let the spray pound me until I felt the muscles unwind.

"I wanted to just close my eyes and forget but I had learned better a long time ago. The dead linger there for quite a while.

"I pulled on the heavy burgundy robe that an ex had given me and went to the kitchen. I took a paper bag out from between the stove and the cupboard, popped it open and went back to the living room.

"I made quick work of emptying the pockets of the clothes I had been wearing out onto the coffee table and shoved the whole kit, shoes included, into the bag. I could still smell the gunpowder. And the blood. I folded the top down, carried the bag to the trash chute in the hallway and tossed it in. Back in my rooms I washed my hands again then poured myself a stiff drink."

-   *When the Clock Strikes Dead*
    Jud Carson, P.I.

*****

'Sarge' didn't bother to pretend when he came to the guard post at Templehof Central Airport. He simply showed his identification, signed an entry on the form held by the sentry, leaned over to kiss Paula on the cheek and turned to lead them back to his room. By the time that they arrived he had been briefed by the two of them and tasked by Jerome. Sarge tapped on the door across the hall and whispered to the young man who answered.

Sarge had asked another neighbor to scoot

down for some chow for his guests and they had just settled in when there was a knock on the door and a piece of paper slid under it. A small photograph followed the slip. Sarge picked them both up and, without bothering to read or even glance at them, handed both over to Jerome.

"You going to want some back up?" he asked.

Jerome shook his head. "I'm going to have to cross over again. The story is that our guy is on vacation in the East."

"Sure you wouldn't want some company? I know all of the right places to eat and drink," Sarge offered again."

Jerome shook his head. "This is straight up my alley," he said.

"Would that be the *Alley of Darkness, Alley of Death*?" Sarge asked with a grin.

Jerome rolled his eyes and groaned. "Don't remind me of that terrible thing!"

Sarge shrugged. "I kind of liked it," he said. "But I won't mention it again if you sign my copy."

"You've got a copy of that? I thought that I had bought them all and burned them."

Sarge held up a hand for him to wait, went to his footlocker and lifted the top tray, setting it aside. He reached in and retrieved the worn paperback and handed it to Jerome. "Got a pen?" he asked.

Jerome retrieved Daisy's lucky pen from his inside pocket, flipped the book open and scrawled "To Sarge – Thanks to all you heroes at TCA – Jud Carson" inside. E handed the book back. "I think that you'd like my new one, *When the Clock Strikes Dead* better."

"I'll look for it," Sarge promised. Then he

reached back into the footlocker and took out a small leather case. "I think you might find a use for these," he said, tugging the zipper back to reveal the thin, black, metal bits inside.

Jerome nodded his thanks and slipped the case into his jacket pocket. He turned and reached for Paula's hand. "I'll see you soon," he said.

When he turned back Sarge had produced a wad of German marks. "I think you're going to need this, too."

"Paula will see to it that you get paid back," Jerome said.

Sarge smirked and opened the door. "Let's just make sure that you put it back in my hand," he said. "Jer – " he glanced at Paula but she seemed to not have noticed. "Jud – this is Berlin. Don't trust anybody."

"Does that go for you, too?" Jerome asked with a wry smile.

"That goes especially for him," Paula laughed.

"Stop complaining," Sarge said. "You got your car back."

"Painted hot pink."

They continued their conversation even as Jerome closed the door behind him.

*****

Leaving the base gate Jerome followed Sarge's directions to and was soon standing in front of 'Snoopy's'. Good, solid, American rock music invited him in. Instead he turned and hailed a passing cab, handing the slip of paper over to the driver as he settled in. In the passing lights he studied the photograph of Berrin Schumann. The note that accompanied the photo reported that Schumann was supposed to be on a short vacation.

Chapter Thirteen

Excerpt, Daily Read File:
Tuesday, 9 November 1989
BBC Monitoring/FBIS

(Berlin, FRG) In an apparent mistake that has taken both the East and the West by surprise, Günter Schabowski, the current unofficial spokesman for the Socialist Unity Party of Germany (GDR) has announced in a press conference broadcast live that new travel rules are being implemented immediately. East Germans living in East Berlin will be permitted to cross into West German with proper permissions. Asked by American journalist Tom Brokaw (NBC) when these changes would take effect, the spokesman hesitated then replied, "As far as I know effective immediately, without delay".

By the end of the 7PM West German news broadcasts thousands of East Germans were waiting at the four border crossings located in the Eastern sector along the Berlin Wall. By 10:45PM they were joined by thousands more and, with border guards reluctant to act, and, reportedly, no higher echelon officers willing to order the use of deadly force, the borders were opened and thousands of East Berliners rushed across the border into the arms of loved ones and strangers waiting on the other side of the once-Iron Curtain.

*****

The opening of the border and the chaos that accompanied it made crossing into the East a less stressful proposition. Still, Jerome's heart pounded as he handed the slip of paper to the cab driver who seemed to be more upset that he had a fare that would take him away from the border and its crush of humanity than he was glad to have a fare. His attitude changed slightly for the better when Jerome gave him a glimpse of the German marks that he would be paid with. Western marks. Hard marks.

He reached through the open front passenger window, opened the rear door and held it while Jerome climbed into the Volga. A moment later the Soviet-made car coughed to life and began its way slowly and laboriously up the street, swimming against the tide of East Germans who continued to stream toward the checkpoint.

They travelled in silence, the driver studying Jerome as they left the crowds and entered streets without lights. I shouldn't have let him see all of that money, Jerome thought. If I don't show up back in the West no one would even know where to start looking for me. He scrunched back deeper into the shadows of the small back seat and felt his heart begin to pound harder.

They made slow but steady progress for several minutes, passing in and out of better and less lighted areas. A small sign announced Potsdam and captured Jerome's attention. This had been the scene of one of the most important conferences of the century. He remembered the black and white photo in his world history book: Stalin, Churchill, and FDR.

"Potsdam," the driver muttered. A few minutes later he pointed toward an ancient city gate that stood as a silent sentinel in the dark. "Platz," he said. Then, in English, as though he were conducting a tour: "The city market."

It was only a few minutes later that the driver stopped a block from Jerome's destination and pointed toward the lights that shown like an island of civility in a sea of inhospitality. Across the street was a subway stop. He turned the key in the ignition and the Volga stopped coughing and rattling. He pointed at himself and then down. He would wait. Jerome handed him forty marks. He held up three more twenty mark bills, folded them and tucked them into his own shirt pocket. The driver looked from the bills in his hand, then toward those hidden in his pocket, and finally directly at Jerome. He nodded once.

Jerome slipped up the street, inside the hotel and up the flight of stairs that embraced the eastern wall without pausing at the desk where the night clerk sat engrossed with the flickering black and white images of the border only a few miles away. He climbed to the third floor and glanced down the hallway before making his way to the door at the far end.

He studied the gap between the bottom of the door and the carpet. There was no light. He listened with his ear turned toward and close to the door. There was no sound. He pulled the small leather case from his pocket and opened it, then eased three of the pieces of blackened steel from their places. One piece slid into the keyhole of the door and pressed down, a second eased past the first and locked into place. He held the two of them with one hand and then inserted the third. The last pick pressed up and when it gave the extra fraction of an inch Jerome pressed the door handle down, swung the door open and quickly slipped into the darkened room. He let the door settle back into place and ran his hand along the wall, flicking on the light switch and scanning the room. A set of keys had been tossed on the nightstand. He picked them up and counted. Four. A car key, one that might be to a strong box. Two that looked like door keys. He frowned. Why two?

A quick search turned up little of interest. One empty suitcase and a packed video camera bag. The drawers were as empty as the suitcase. So much for Berrin taking a short vacation. Why bring a camera bag, he wondered as he made his way around the room. It made some sense. It, unlike the suitcase, would already be packed and it would be something that people would expect to see a traveler to have.

The bathroom was German sterile and neatly arranged with only a few personal belongings. Taking the bar of soap from the sink and the other from the bath he returned to the bedroom. Quickly unwrapping the bars he set them on the nightstand beside Berrin's keys. A moment later he had made impressions of both of the house keys on the bars of soap. He wiped the keys clean of the evidence and slipped the bars into his jacket pocket. The keys were replaced and he moved to the other side of the room.

He retrieved the video camera from the closet's top shelf. A quick inspection showed that, although there was no cassette in the camera itself, there was one in a side pocket.

He closed the closet door behind him and scanned the room again. A small cabinet was fixed in the corner of the far wall, the pale light from the street painting a ribbon down its front. A pair of aristocrats danced on the front door panel. Jerome turned the fragile-looking handle and the painted door swung open with a slight tug. Inside, resting on a packet of folded papers was the object of his search: a small, dull black automatic pistol nearly hidden in the shadows of the cabinet's interior. For an instant he considered how he would pick it up, then remembered that finger-prints are, despite crime-drama lore, rarely recovered from handguns. He reached in and retrieved the pistol.

Glancing around the room he found what he was looking for. A small couch fitted out with three of what his mother had called "decorator pillows" stood on the far side of the room. A small end table with a built-in reading lamp was positioned at the end nearest the bed. Before moving across the room he released the clip from the well of the automatic's handle and quickly inspected it. Fully loaded. He replaced the clip and turned the weapon so that he could see the ejector. Gently easing back the slide he could see the brass cartridge seated in the firing chamber. Berrin was not taking any chances that he might pull the hammer on an empty tube. He released the slide and moved to the end table.

He set the gun down and hurried back to the closet. He took the camera bag from its place and ran his hand along the shelf looking for something to support it. When he accepted that Berrin had not brought a tri-pod, he flipped the camera's on switch, scratched the plastic wrap on the VHS tape and opened its package. He dropped the wrapping onto the closet floor and kicked it back into the far corner.

He positioned the camera on the table pointed toward the opposite end and squatted down to look at the field of view he would have. Too low. The high edge of the couch completely blocked the camera's view. He looked the room over again. No books to speak of. There was a decorative box on the other end table, but it would be too tall. Then, on the bedside table he saw the box of tissues. He grabbed it, perched the camera atop and checked it again. Too low. For a moment he looked around the room, even patting his own pockets in hopes of finding something that would produce a pedestal of adequate height. Nothing.

He moved to the bed and sat down, trying to gain a new perspective on the room. His left hand dropped to the table that had recently held the tissue box. He looked at it again. A drawer was built in below the tabletop. A pull on the brass handle opened the white-paper lined drawer.

"Well, Paula, here's hoping that the united workers of the world will set you free," he whispered as he took the copy of *Das Capital* from the drawer and rushed back to his task. Combined, the box and book were too tall, but he pulled a handful of tissues from the box, placed them in a stack on the table and put the book on top. Too tall. Another try and he had accomplished his goal: the lens would have a clear and unobstructed view of his improvised test range.

He started recording and picked up the pistol, holding it before the camera's eye to record the serial number etched into the metal below the hammer. Then, making sure that the pistol never left the field of view, he moved back to the far end of the couch where he placed two of the hard pillows on top of one another and pushed the barrel of the gun against the top cushion. Taking a shallow breath and holding it, glanced at the camera then concentrated on the gun again. The long pull of the trigger broke at last and a muffled "Buhh!" sounded. The spent shell ejected from the side port and arced onto the seat of the couch a half a foot closer to the camera. There was very little kick but the smell of cordite and gunpowder plumed and quickly spread. The muzzle flash had ignited the cotton batting and Jerome quickly patted the fire out before it could burst into open flame.

Leaving the gun on top of the pillows he used a thumb and index finger to pick up the spent shell. He held it at various angles in front of the camera then, using his other hand retrieved a Sharpie from his inside pocket. He bit the cap off and wrote his initials and the date on the side of the shell. Done, he moved the casing, making sure that his writing was visible closer to the camera and held it there for several seconds. Finally he turned the empty brass cartridge so that he could capture the image of the firing pin impact and the inscription around it. Satisfied, he pocketed the shell, re-capped the pen and put it away.

Going back to the end of the couch he searched through the top and bottom pillows, finally sticking a finger into the hole in the couch that had been made by the bullet. He had to struggle and finally tear the hole wider, but the couch gave up the slug.

For a moment he considered how he could mark it as he had the shell casing. There was no way to do it, he conceded. Time to get out. And past time. He pressed the button that opened the cassette door, removed the tape and slipped it into his coat pocket. Then he switched off the camera, re-cased and restored it. The tissues were stuffed back into the box and it and the Communist bible were returned to their proper places. The damage to the pillows and couch would be another matter.

In the closet he found a plastic bag for the hotel guest's catered laundry. He stuffed the two damaged pillows inside it and tied it closed. The third pillow was positioned over the torn couch fabric. Things looked right enough, he supposed, but there was no ignoring the smell of spent gunpowder. In the bathroom he found a bottle of Berrin's cologne. A couple of sprays in the main room did little to eliminate the odor. He gave the couch a few more sprays, returned the cologne to its shelf and a moment later had replaced the gun in the cabinet.

"None of this is going to fool anybody," he said to himself. "But maybe it will be enough to buy a little time and keep 'em confused."

The night clerk glanced up as Jerome made his way down the final flight of stairs and left the lobby. He paused under the light and looked up the street to where the Volga still sat. Then he crossed the street and descended the stairs into the subway. In the center of the platform he found the phone stand.

He tried the number for Dare and Claire but there was no answer. He had done too good of a job convincing them to take time off. When he needed the lawyer to be on the job he was out dancing or romancing his own wife. More proof that lawyers couldn't be trusted, he thought.

He picked up the receiver, paid and dialed again.

"I need your help," Jerome said when Daisy answered her phone.

"Of course," she answered. His tone of voice hadn't registered yet and hers was as light and airy as it had been the last time that he had kissed her and wished her a good day.

"Not so fast," he went on. "This means that you have to meet me in Potsdam."

He waited while the reality sank in. Daisy was in Steglitz and Steglitz was in the West, where people were trying to get to. Potsdam as in the East. Where people were trying to get out of.

"You need this?" she asked.

"Yes," he said. "I do. I can't get a hold of anyone else that I can trust." Again he waited.

Daisy took a deep breath. "I will do what you ask," she said.

"There is a market," he said, on the way to Sanssouci. There is a gate there. It's pretty obvious – you can't miss it – I will meet you there."

"I will leave now," Daisy said. Her voice bore the tone of determination. She would do this thing – no matter how dangerous, because he asked. But she would not consider the question of risk. That might change her decision.

"Daisy," he said, "they aren't stopping anyone on the border. Anyone crossing into the East is not going to have any problem. I wouldn't ask if I thought that there was any alternative."

"They are not stopping anyone on the border," Daisy repeated, then added, "now. This can change without warning. Being caught on the East without papers is a very dangerous thing."

"If you don't think that – " he began.

"I am leaving now," she said, cutting him off. For an instant they both held their silence, then, gently, Daisy returned the telephone receiver to its cradle.

Jerome cursed himself for calling her and left the booth.

Chapter Fourteen

Jerome looked at the photograph again and back at the man who had just emerged from the hotel across the street. Satisfied that they were the same man, he began to move up his side of the thoroughfare, keeping a safe distance between Berrin Schumann and himself. If Schumann knew he was being followed, he did not show it, but then, that would be expected, Jerome told himself. This was his country, his city. His street. And the game was his, too. There was no telling how long the German had been playing it. Jerome only knew one thing: there weren't any rules. He followed Schumann across the street and into the UBahn. He waited at the far end of the platform until the train rolled in and stopped.

A few riders got off. Mostly kids with wannabe American punk styles and over-priced American jeans. Schumann got on toward the front of the train. Jerome got on at the back. The train left the station with a lurch and he was nearly knocked off his feet. A pair of strong hands steadied him and held him until he had secured a hold on the railing.

Jerome looked into the face of the young man who had helped him. Short hair and clean shaven. Jeans and a cowboy hat. He could be an off-duty American G.I., Jerome thought.

"Gut?" the stranger asked.

Jerome nodded once and turned back toward the front of the train. He glanced up at the map that showed the train's route. If Schumann didn't leave the train in three more stops they would be back in the West.

The German with the Stetson left the subway when it reached the last stop before the Allied Sector and Jerome stepped out onto the platform after him. But Schumann did not emerge. Jerome moved two cars up. Now he was only one car behind Schumann. Jerome sighed in frustration. Daisy was on her way into the East to meet him at the Sanssouci market. If he followed Berrin she would be there alone and for no reason. On the other hand he couldn't afford to lose his quarry now.

Jerome heard the warning tone that indicated that the train would be leaving in seconds. He glanced back at the clock that hung suspended above the ticket booth. The driver from the Volga was making his way back up the stairs and out of the station.

"Please step forward." The nudge to his back left no doubt that there was no option. Without turning around he knew that the small man with the hard eyes and harder fists was behind him. But it was not a fist that poked into his still-tender ribs.

Jerome stepped back through the doors and moved to the train waiting on the opposite track. He could see Schumann cross over as well and enter the car in front of him. In a moment they had retreated from the border and were heading back toward Potsdam once more.

Chapter Fifteen

Notebook 24, Entry 25

"I could hear the penguins ice skating out in the living room before I was fully awake. Or maybe it was mice, all decked out in patent leathers and black tie at a dance. No, not that, either. My right hand moved out toward the bedside table, knocked over the water glass which fell onto the thickly carpeted floor as I continued to grope for the butt of my automatic.

"I could hear Stan laughing. 'Where's the roscoe?' he mocked.

"I forced my eyes open and drew a deep breath. The elephants in the living room were rearranging the furniture and I didn't like the way that they were doing it.

"I sat up, checked the light in the room – nothing but a little bit of street light seeping in – and swung my legs out from beneath the covers. I came fully awake when my feet hit the puddle of water on the carpet.

"I reached down and pulled the sheathed KA-BAR combat knife from under the bed. I unsnapped the strap and cleared the blade, moved to the door and listened. No penguins. No mice. No elephants. But there was someone out there, going through things and they didn't want to be noticed. I checked the bottom of the door. No light shown through.

"They were using a flashlight, then. Good. I knew

the lay-out better than they would. It also meant that, if I was fast enough, I wouldn't be facing a weapon. Since my un-invited guest had to have one hand for the flashlight and one hand to search with I would have a big advantage. I gripped the handle of the door and eased it open.

"The flash of the light swung up – I threw the knife sheath at the place I guessed would be the head and charged. I held my left forearm up like I was a Roman centurion with a shield and connected with a body. I drove forward, pushing the burglar backward toward the front door. When we slammed to a stop I kept the pressure of my left forearm up, pinning the intruder, and brought the tip of the combat knife up to a throat – the back of my hand came to rest against – the curve – of a breast.

"I kept the knife in place, dropped my left arm and found the light switch. The overhead bulbs glared and Elaine Merriman's frightened eyes stared back at me. I could feel her breast heave against the back of my hand as I continued to rest the knife tip just below her delicate chin.

"Then I took a step back and looked down at the knife in my hand. The hand was trembling and for some reason or reasons that I didn't understand then and still don't I found myself laughing at the sight. I even looked back at Elaine and nodded from her to the spectacle so that she could get a laugh, too. But she wasn't laughing. She was still panting. She was still pressing her back against the door. A single pin-head of crimson, like a rose blooming in the snow, had welled up where the tip of the knife had rested against the alabaster of her throat.

"Seeing that cut off my laughter. I stumbled back from her and managed to make my way to the chair by the wall cabinet.

"I dropped down onto the cushions and let my hand that still held the knife drape over the arm rest. A second later my grip relaxed and the knife fell, blade first, down to stick in the floor. I lowered my head and rested it in the palm of my left hand.

"I could hear Elaine's breathing begin to quiet and she was moving away from the door, toward me. She knelt in front of me, curled her legs underneath herself and rested her head on my thighs.

"They – they told me you were, they said that you had been – " she choked back tears.

"No," I managed, "I'm not. I wasn't. A lot of other guys were, but not me."

"I'm so grateful," she gasped. "I don't know what I would have done if you had been – "

"Killed? Murdered? Whacked? Taken for a ride?"

"Yes!" she sobbed.

"I pushed her back and stood up.

"It's time to drop the 'damsel in distress' act, Love. It doesn't suit you."

"I don't understand, Jud, what do you mean?"

"I mean that I don't believe you. And I don't think that Danny Granger believed you, either."

"Her sobs stopped at the mention of Granger's name. She stood and straightened her clothes. "Granger?" she asked. Her eyes showed question marks but the rest of her confessed that she was lying.

"Yeah," I said, warming up to the subject. "Danny Granger. The first guy that you were told about by those people whose opinion you value so much. If they sent you to me it would have been after you had already seen him."

"I stepped over to the cabinet where I keep the hooch and poured one, downed it and poured a second just in case the first needed reinforcements.

"She bit her lower lip and was working her story up when I decided that one slug wasn't going to settle the issue for me. I tossed off the second and pushed the glass away.

"You've got to trust me, Jud," she said. Her voice was desperate but I wasn't listening to her words so much as I was watching her eyes and her hands; both were as busy as a chippie's on the night that the fleet comes in. Her hands twisted and untwisted the belt of the trench coat that she wore and her eyes skitted around the room.

"Trust you? When did trust come into this relationship? You've done nothing but hand me lies and promises and promises that we both knew were lies. You should have told me that you hired him," I said. "That would have been the smart play."

"She nodded and bit her lower lip. I might have spanked her and sent her home if she'd been anyone else. If the case had been any other case. If he had been any one else on a long list of others. Well, she wasn't. It wasn't. He wasn't.

"You knew that Brighton was in town looking for

you. So you hired a P.I. to hold the letter and went into hiding."

"She nodded, her eyes flitting up to check my reaction, then they went back to their dance.

"Yes, but when I got a buyer for the letter I went to get it back." She leaned toward me and lowered her eyes, her left hand extended to lay her palm against my chest. She tried to move closer but stopped when she felt me stiffen my back and move away a fraction of an inch.

"I had to do it, Jud," she whispered with a slight crack in her voice. Gone were the sultry tones of seduction. She was playing for sympathy and the orchestra was just tuning up.

"He – he – " She shook her head as though shedding a bad memory. Then she looked up at me again. "He tried to – you know?"

"I could feel the ice water hit the top of my head and run down my spine. I had been hoping against hope that she would have something – anything – that I could tell myself might be believable. Maybe even true. But this story didn't have a chance. I looked away from her.

"Jud, you understand, don't you?"

"I nodded. "I understand," I said. "You killed him. But not because he tried to rape you."

"He did!" She insisted. "It was terrible! I was so scared and I just – I just – I didn't even think!"

"Oh, you thought, all right," I answered. "And you thought wrong. You got it into your pretty little head that Danny was selling you out and had set you up. Or maybe you just didn't want to pay him what you owed him. That would be an easy choice for you to make. So you killed him. But you couldn't find the letter. Then you figured that you could get me to get your letter back. Now you think that I'll believe anything that you say. Because you know that I want to."

"She looked up at me and a ghost of a smile kissed her lips.

"Yeah, I'd love to believe you," I said. I let my eyes and voice go dull. "But I don't."

"Her look asked where and how she had messed up.

"Danny Granger had a lover," I said. "And if you had done your homework you would have known that your story wouldn't fly."

"It wouldn't be the first time that a man – "

"My open hand snapped up and froze in mid-air. Her eyes were wide and her open mouth stopped working.

"Yeah, men get tempted," I snarled. "But you couldn't tempt Granger. See, Danny's lover is an entertainer named Dixie LaBlanc. But before taking to the stage Dixie LaBlanc was known as David Patterson. The only interest that Danny had in you was that stash of century notes. And in getting the job done – because that's the kind of op he was."

"She turned ashen and edged away toward the settee.

"I thought that he was going to sell me out," she said softly. "I thought that he had made his own deal with Jeffrey." She eased herself down onto the seat and for an instant it seemed that she might just keep going – dissolve into the cushions and then down through the floor itself.

"So you went to his place," I began again.

"She nodded. "I told him that I wanted the letter back but he said that it wasn't there. I – "

"You tried to scare him."

"She nodded.

"And you scared him to death."

"He told me that he didn't like having guns pointed at him. He just kept walking toward me…"

"I waived a hand to cut her off. I didn't need to hear the rest of that.

"And last night you saw that box of Granger's things in my room. You'd seen the photo of all of us at his place so you knew whose it was. You saw the pawn ticket and you figured out where the letter was stashed. You figured that you could make a deal with Brighton. So you told him that if I was out of the picture you would produce the letter and the two of you could divvy up the proceeds. You're the reason that I have three more dead men to answer for."

"I didn't tell him to have you killed," she said softly. "I didn't want that."

"I shrugged. "Maybe you did, and maybe you didn't. The difference doesn't amount to much."

"I slumped back against the wall and sighed. She lowered her chin and stared at her shoes. For a long time we avoided looking at one another.

"I wondered how long it would take before she

decided to play the next card: pulling a small caliber automatic out of her coat pocket and settling for the letter – or the pawn ticket – before calling us quits.

"I decided to spare us both before it got any uglier. "The ticket isn't here," I said. "Neither is the letter. And they won't be."

"Then I pushed off from the wall and made my way across the room to stand beside her. I put a hand on her hair. "If I thought about this long enough and hard enough I could maybe come up with a story that would get you out of this mess." I took her shoulders in both hands and squeezed just a little.

"But not without putting my neck in a noose and your hand on the trapdoor lever." I searched her face for some sign of understanding but all that was written there was her plea for pity. Well, in my years I had learned that when it is time for pity it is too late. I knew that she would never be able to step outside of her own desires long enough to see it any other way. And I knew that, in time, I could get over my desire for her to do just that.

"I can give you an hour," I said as I moved away. "After that…"

When the Clock Strikes Dead
Jud Carson, P.I.

*****

When they left the subway train they were back at the same station where Jerome had placed the call to Daisy. Schumann continued to move ahead of

Jerome and his escort. None of the three seemed to be concerned. They were safe behind the Berlin Wall. The incongruity made him smile wryly. Safe behind the Berlin Wall. Safe in East Berlin. Berrin glanced back at the three of them then pointed to the bus stop between the Potsdam market and Schumann's hotel. The entourage made their way across the street and mounted the double-decker when it stopped. Berrin Schumann sat in the front and Jerome brushed against him as they passed.

Minutes later Berrin stood and waited at the exit doors for the bus to come to a halt on a darkened street. Across the avenue Jerome could see a tall, arched gateway that led into deeper darkness. The fear that had been mounting in the pit of Jerome's stomach now threatened to rush up through his chest and burst forth. It was the realization that even if he were to find a cop and could somehow explain in fluent German what was going on – what he knew was going to happen – it wouldn't make any difference. He was, after all, in the wrong place and with the wrong company.

He wondered if and when anyone would know what had happened to him. Sweet Billy Madrid. I should have tried to make a break for it back when I was almost in the West, he thought. There wasn't going to be any cavalry coming around the bend to save him. A run now was certain death. Of course, later was pretty much the same thing, now.

Berrin had stopped at a short stone wall that bordered a rising slope. "Let me officially welcome you to the German Democratic Republic," he said graciously. "I trust that you will be staying with us for some time."

The short man behind Jerome chuckled.

"Perhaps you would be so kind as to show me your papers," Berrin went on. When Jerome did not respond he clucked in mock seriousness. "No papers? This is very serious. I suspect that you are a Western agitator who has infiltrated our glorious Socialist Republic to instigate anti-revolutionary disturbances." He smiled, more, Jerome, realized for the short man's benefit than for his own.

"Do these chuckle-heads know that you have been playing both ends against the middle?" Jerome asked at last.

Berrin's reaction was unguarded and showed his shock.

"Vas?" the short man asked.

"The bear here has been racking it in from both – "

"Enough!" Berrin said fiercely cutting him off.

Jerome glanced from him to the short man. "Seems pretty touchy. Did I kick some glorious socialist wound?"

Even in the dim light Jerome could see that the short man was looking at Berrin somewhat differently now. And he could tell that Berrin was seeing the same thing.

"I wonder if he has been cutting you boys in on the take," Jerome said slowly. It was a calculated risk, he knew, but then, every breath now was just that. "Did you two get your passports in order for the great migration? I'm sure that Berrin here is going to need somebody to carry his bags when the Wall comes a'tumblin' down."

The short man was looking more at Berrin now than he was at Jerome. That was good. Not good enough, but good.

"You two stay here," Berrin said, taking control.

"Got some cards? We can play gin while we wait," Jerome said to the short man. Then, to Berrin, "Are you going to be long? I wanted to order a pizza." He glanced at the short man again who was studying him quizzically, then a smile began to creep from the corners of his thin lips.

Berrin put his hand in his jacket pocket, brought it out enough for Jerome to recognize the gun that he had handled in the hotel room. "I believe that you are familiar with this," he said. He nodded toward the bend further up the street. "Time to go," he said, gesturing with the gun. "Now."

"You guys wait here," Jerome said to the others. "I think that Berrin wants to be alone with me. Romantic devil."

The short man shook his head as through trying to avoid laughter. Jerome could hear him speaking to his companion as he and his captor began to move away.

The sidewalk and the grade of the walkway combined to make their progress slow. Jerome could feel every blow that the short man had landed and he struggled to keep his mind seeking avenues for escape. He had managed, by luck, to separate Berrin from the others. That was progress. But there was no doubt that Berrin did not intend to be making the trip back down the hill with Jerome.

"Mind telling me where the hell we are going?" he asked.

"This is Sanssouci," Berrin answered. "German palace of Fredrick the Great."

"Sanssouci, huh?" Jerome mused. "'No

worries'."

"The palace of rest," Berrin said.

"You are a sick bastard," Jerome sighed.

"I thought that you would appreciate the twist of it."

They had turned up the broad driveway. A small guard shack stood beside a set of black iron gates. There was no guard. The gates were chained closed.

"End of the line?" Jerome asked, half turning toward Berrin. The German nodded toward the gates. "I believe that you can slip through. Slowly."

"I don't know – I've been hitting your good German beer," Jerome said, patting his stomach.

"You'll manage. Go."

Jerome approached the gates and pressed against one of them. A gap opened and widened when he adjusted the chain to achieve its greatest width. "I'm going to have to charge you for the dry cleaning," Jerome said, pushing through the opening.

"Step back," Berrin said. He had the gun out now and had leveled its barrel at Jerome's midsection. He glanced between Jerome and the gate, moving slowly forward and using his left hand to press against the gate. With the other hand he kept Jerome under the pressure of the gun.

"They're on to you, you know," Jerome said.

"I am not so sure," Berrin said. "A bit further back, please." He extended the hand holding the gun through the gate and stepped forward. "I think that you will find that your government will be quite happy to have someone such as myself to provide them with insights into the working of their enemy." He glanced down and brought his empty hand up to free a jacket button that had become wedged against the iron of the gate.

"Maybe," Jerome said. "But it won't be you."

Too late Berrin turned his full attention back to Jerome who had raised his left leg and kicked hard into the gate. The impact sent a shock wave through Berrin who grunted and struggled to keep his grip on the pistol. The gate had smacked into his head and he was pressed sharply between the two sets of bars. A rib cracked. His breath was driven out. The gun hand dipped. Jerome disappeared into the shadows.

Rabbit and wolf, Jerome chanted in his mind as he pushed himself to continue to climb up the incline. The wolf runs for his dinner but the rabbit runs for his life. Yeah, well, the wolf is pretty determined not to starve to death, too. His feet moved from pavement to grass. There was a building of some sort to his right. Won't be open, he thought. Break in. No, it could be alarmed. That's all I need – more guys with guns looking for me. And they'd all be on his side.

He paused and listened. Berrin was behind him, alright. His footsteps were more cautious but he would be determined. If he let Jerome get away he was going to have more problems than explaining his expense account.

Jerome skirted the building and found himself on a gravel walking path. The shadows painted on other shadows gave him a rough outline of the building. Might be the main hacienda, he thought. Maybe not. What passed for a palace around here? Frederick may have been German but it was a cinch that he would have modeled his get-away on a French layout.

He wished again that he had made more of an

effort in high school French. They had gone on an eight-day trip to France. He had gone to summer school.

He followed the path and then found a way down over wide terraces. Now his heart raced as he realized that he was much too obvious. There was no cover here. Behind him he heard Berrin's footsteps as his pursuer stepped onto the gravel path. He nearly lost his balance and tumbled head first down the stepped terraces as he began to race downward. Berrin must have heard him, he thought; he is right behind me and it won't be long until I feel that little pill that I have been writing about all this time. He had reached the bottom and dashed behind a pillar on his right.

A wide fountain stood at the center of the final level. He longed for a cool drink. In your dreams, he chastised himself.

Yeah, there's Berrin, he thought. And me without so much as a slingshot. He panted, took a deep breath, exhaled it forcefully and moved off to the right. There were trees there. Maybe a place to hide. Maybe something to use as an equalizer. Berrin had slowed a bit. Then, realizing that Jerome had made a break for the deeper cover, he picked up his pace again.

Jerome stepped off the path and tried to make himself small. He could see Berrin's shadow as the man followed him. I could jump him when he gets even with me, he thought. Or wait until he goes by and then do it. Or hope that he keeps going and double back. Berrin had stopped and was listening. His head tilted first to one side and then to the other.

He knows that I haven't gone too far. He knows

that I am close, Jerome thought. He felt the stiffness settle into his knees where he knelt. He's going to spot me and shoot me like a dog, he thought. I wonder how ol' Emperor Fred would like that.

Berrin took a step forward; then he took another.

"You are in a very dangerous place," Berrin began. His voice was low. He knew that Jerome was nearby. He stopped and listened. Then, "I am sure that we can work out something that will satisfy us both. That is why I brought you here alone. I did not want those Stasi thugs to know what we have to say to one another."

Three more short steps. He was just abreast of Jerome now. He stopped and listened. Oh, God, Jerome thought. Don't let him hear me breathing! Should I hold my breath? If I do, how long before I am gasping for a breath and then gasping out my last one? He tried to keep his breaths short and controlled.

Berrin took two more steps. Should he leap out now? Smash the German on the side of his head? Lock his arms around his neck and squeeze and keep squeezing until the man stopped fighting back? Then a little more until he stopped breathing. Then maybe a little more for Paula.

Berrin took two more steps. Now he would have a warning if Jerome moved. Jerome waited and felt his joints continue to grow cold and stiff.

Berrin seemed to relax although the gun was still held up in front of him. He moved more quickly, though not hurriedly, to the center of the walkway where other paths intersected from the left and right. Jerome presumed that the path that had led him here also continued out on the other side.

Cautiously, slowly, he stood and stretched his aching legs. The chill and damp of the night air had begun to settle in upon him. He longed for his old trench coat. And for the neighborhoods of San Francisco. And for its enveloping, obscuring fog.

Berrin had stopped and was looking about. "We won't be leaving until we have made an agreement of some sort," he said. "I am willing to compromise – I am a civilized man, as are you. Come, let us work together to discover a mutually agreeable answer to this dilemma."

"You killed your uncle and pinned it on his girlfriend," Jerome whispered.

Berrin seemed to flinch, but it was from the shock of hearing his voice, not the words, Jerome realized. He would try to keep his intended victim talking while he searched for him based on the direction of his voice. Good luck, he thought, you're not a damned bat. Speaking softly out here and being able to move in the shadows of the trees would give him an advantage over the German.

"And you know this how?"

"You switched the barrels. All you had to do was make sure that the gun you used was the same make and model as the one that Florian had given Paula. That was easy. And I have to admit, it was pretty damned clever. But it wasn't quite clever enough."

He knew that Berrin wanted to ask him why it was not a better plan, but they were both more concerned about the real issue – Jerome's life or death.

"But the fact is that the firing pin strike mark

from her gun is going to be different than the one on yours. And when the slide kicks out the spent shell it leaves a mark, too. The ejector marks don't match up," Jerome said. "And when they check the breach face marks on shells from her gun, they won't match the shells at the scene, either. But those marks will all match up with your gun."

"That's unfortunate," Berrin said. "That means that this gun will never again travel to the West. Still, so long as the polizei have a gun barrel that matches the bullet, and a suspect with the gun that it came from, there is not so much reason for them to look further."

Sonofabitch, Jerome thought. This damned thing just keeps grinding finer. An hour a go he had to evade. Half an hour ago he had to escape. Now he was going to have to go home with a prize.

"Good. Well done. Now we can put this aside."

"You killed the girl, too," Jerome went on. "Ana – Anda – the Kurtz woman." He tossed his words carelessly to see how they would be caught.

"Andelisa Kurtz," Berrin corrected. Jerome had managed to hit a nerve. He could hear it in the man's lowered tone and the edge that he had in his voice when correcting her name.

"Yeah, you ought to get kicked to death by some of your best friends for that one."

"She knew that I knew things," Berrin said simply. Jerome thought that he could detect some regret or at least sadness over the way that things had turned out for the woman.

"You couldn't get her to pinky-swear to keep her mouth shut?"

Berrin did not respond, knowing now that

Jerome was baiting him.

"You know, that was a cold-son-of-a-bitch thing to do," Jerome said softly "I'd like to see you dead for that alone."

Again, Berrin did not answer.

"I think that it was the Throckmorton thing that really set you up," Jerome went on. "Let me see if I can get this figured out." He began to edge around to his right which put him in deeper cover but might also bring him around to the other side of the clearing. It had become obvious to him that Berrin's plan was to merely keep him here, relatively pinned down, until the sun revealed him in a few hours. If they were to have company by that time, so much the better for Berrin.

Escape would be pointless, even if Jerome could manage it. He was in the East and would be quickly captured by Berrin or his allies. The options had run out. He could almost hear Jud Carson chastising him for having let himself be trapped, unarmed and nearly out of time.

"How do you know about him?" Berrin asked with genuine curiosity.

"He was a spy, too, right?"

"Yes, and of the old school."

"Which means that he was a proper English gent who just happened to be playing both ends against the middle. And you taught him a new trick or two." Jerome was near to the far edge of the narrow stand of trees.

"Everyone has a price," Berrin said nonchalantly. "I suspect that those I work with could even meet yours."

"Maybe. But then, I'm pretty cheap to keep."

Jerome stopped. From where he was now he could not see Berrin. He listened. There was the sound of gravel being shifted, but it could be just the idle movement of a stationary vigil.

"So he had crossed over the Rubicon," Jerome said softly. "Did you go to him, or did he look you up?"

"We had mutual friends. When I expressed an interest in – " the German hesitated, trying to think of a term that would convey meaning without applying undesirable stigma to his choices.

"Being a traitor and spy against your country?" Jerome offered.

Berrin sighed but went on. "I was told to contact Sir Thomas. He had made that decision long before it became a question for me."

"So the Commies already had a handler for the new dog," Jerome put in. He could sense that his needling was no longer having an effect, but it gave him a small bit of satisfaction.

"So to speak. But, as they say: Beware the dog – he bites! Sir Thomas had decided that the retirement being offered by his superiors was not adequate. He believed that they owed him much more than that for his many years of devoted service."

"So he was working for the Stasi, too."

"'With' is more correct."

"And you were doing the same thing."

"I have always felt that the idea of 'highest bidder' was important in the capitalist nations."

The gravel crunched again, this time Jerome was sure of it. If Berrin did not know just where his prey was, neither did Jerome have a clear idea of where Berrin was.

"And when Throckmorton refused to cover for

you, you exercised your option."

"I do not understand."

"You murdered him," Jerome said more bluntly.

"Me? How can you say such a thing?"

"I have your travel dates. Throckmorton was killed while you were in London and you turned up back in the Fatherland right after his body was discovered."

"I was given no choice."

"You're a traitor. No one forced you into that," Jerome said.

"But, you see, I am a realist," Berrin countered.

"So, with all of this wonderful Marxism hitting the skids it was going to come out that you had been investing in communist war-bonds. That wouldn't look too good for a book seller dedicated to the free enterprise system, right?"

"If – or when, that is, this system collapses, there are going to be many who must answer for having chosen the wrong side."

"And for those of you who picked both sides?"

"This will be more of a problem, yes."

"And your uncle was in the same leaky boat with you?"

"Nein. My uncle was through and through a Cold Warrior who hated the Communists. He hated the Fascists, too. During the war he was a shadow warrior against the Nazis."

"So, why kill him? Inheritance?"

Berrin snorted. He's just off to the left, Jerome thought. If I can get a shot at him before he gets one at me. Rabbit versus rabbit. Wolf versus wolf.

"My uncle was too close to discovering his nephew's secret," Berrin replied. His voice sounded distracted, as though he were concentrating on something entirely different from the conversation.

He knows how close we are, Jerome thought. I should keep my mouth shut.

"He was to be the one that would review the Stasi paid informer files. He would have been the one to come to me."

"And the girl is the one who told you that there was a Stasi informer who could give you away," Jerome said despite himself.

"And Throckmorton refused to end our arrangement. He would have turned me over to the Allies. In his position he could have denied that he was just as guilty as me."

"So you killed them all," Jerome whispered softly. "Three people had to die so that you could have a bigger car. Oh, wait, with me that will make four, right?"

"I know about you, too" Berrin said softly. "I know that your name is not really 'Jud Carson'. "I know that you are not a police man, a detective, or a spy. You are not even a soldier. You never have been." He eased around the corner of the hedge and found himself staring at Jerome in the dull shadows. Only a few feet separated the two men. Berrin's pistol seemed to occupy most of that space.

"You are just another American – meddling in affairs too far beyond you." Berrin eased the muzzle of the gun a bit further away from his body. At this range he hardly needed to concern himself with missing. There would need be only one gentle pull of the trigger, a gunshot muffled by the dense foliage and the sound of a meddling American falling to the well-manicured trail. Berrin smiled ruefully. He adjusted the barrel upward. "And now you will not even be that," he said.

"Wrong," Jerome snapped. He had side-stepped to the left before Berrin could apply the necessary pressure on the trigger. The German tried to correct his aim and to catch Jerome in his sights again but the American had thrust his left hand, palm perpendicular to his wrist, across his own body and locked his fingers onto Berrin's wrist, immobilizing the joint, hand, and gun all at once. Jerome's right hand flashed down, a trail of silver arcing over his left arm and driving down into Berrin's right temple.

When he stepped back an instant later Berrin's gun was in Jerome's left hand and the pen that he driven forcefully into Berrin's skull was gleaming dully, making the man look like some warped unicorn. Berrin stood still for fully a quarter of a minute, his expression first one of shock, then, as his eyes began to lose focus, the look turned to one of acceptance. He dropped heavily to his knees and tried to turn his face toward Jerome but the effort was too much and he took a long, ragged breath.

"Wrong. Again. I'm a *writer*, schmuck," Jerome said softly.

Berrin seemed to nod but could only manage the downward motion of his head. He pitched forward and did not move again.

Jerome felt the bile rise in his throat, burning him and bringing him to his knees beside the dead German. With an effort he rose again, and, turning, he stumbled up the path toward the fountain. He resisted drinking from its stale waters but did wet his handkerchief and patted his face and neck with the cold water. He dropped Berrin's gun into the right hand pocket of his jacket.

*****

Notebook 24, Entry 26

"There are two kinds of sexy – there's the kind that comes from her knowing who she is and how much power she has – and that can be enough to break your stride and have you laid up until she decides otherwise. Then there is the other kind – the kind that doesn't focus on her at all – it's all about you and the way that she makes you feel, not only about her, but about you. And that kind can kill you. Because if it doesn't come through you just might not have anything left. Elaine Merriman had one of those types of sexy. Sally Hemmings had the other."

-   *When the Clock Strikes Dead*
    Jud Carson, P.I.

*****

The sun was beginning to peak from behind the eastern skyline when Jerome finally made his way down across the rolling front lawn of the former imperial palace and retreat. He had nearly lost his footing a dozen times before reaching the cracked and potted sidewalk. Turning right he began the walk down to the city market.

Few cars passed him by. There would not be much traffic here today, he thought. It might be quite some time before Berrin was discovered. By then he intended to be in another country. The sun continued its steady climb and he felt the thirst, weariness, terror, and combined pains of his struggles and injuries when he made the final turn and could see the remains of the gate that still stood at the entrance to the market.

He nearly let himself pick up his pace; he could feel his step become lighter and his spirits buoy but the passing East German polizei car checked his eagerness. Besides, he had no idea if Daisy was still there. She would have been right in assuming that something had kept him from the rendezvous and gone home, back to the West and to safety.

He crossed the street and let his eyes search along the edges of the gate. No one was there. He moved through the gate itself and looked left and right. Perhaps she was resting there, her back to the ancient stones. No, she was not there, either. Despite the rising sun he felt his eyesight dim. The struggle was catching up with him. He longed to be back in San Francisco. He wished that he were in his own bed and the clock alarm was not going to sound for hours – days – to come.

And, while he was at it, he admitted that he wished he had never spoken to Gwendolyn Dean.

Jerome Carstead slumped, his knees nearly buckling and his head coming down to rest on his chest. He considered lowering himself to the cobble stones of the street but did not even seem to have the energy to move from this balanced state and to allow himself to fall.

Somewhere a bird chirped. He managed to open his eyes and saw the magpie that had perched on the arm of a bench a few dozen yards away. It looked at him critically and chirped again. Somewhere he had read that magpies were one of the smartest animals on the planet. He had always wanted to put that somewhere in one of his books. Now he doubted that he would get the chance.

Something on the bench stirred. The magpie chirped and flapped its wings but stood its ground. The stirring became an unfolding and turning toward Jerome. Daisy brought fists to her eyes and rubbed them. She blinked and seemed to suddenly register that he was there.

Jerome willed himself forward but was incapable of moving beyond a slight swaying from left to right. Daisy rose and ran to him, her strong arms catching him just as gravity seemed to have conquered both his resolve and his last reserve of energy.

"You came," he whispered into her hair.

Daisy did not answer, she merely crooned to him.

"You came," he said again.

She nodded. Then her lips brushed his cheek and ear.

"I lost your lucky pen," he said, breathing her in.

"It's all right," she said. "I never liked that pen anyway."

He managed to bring a hand up and touched her hair gently. As he did, he saw the two men entering the market from the other end. One was tall and wide. The other was short and had the build of a welterweight. Jerome felt his knees go weak as he watched them begin to slowly make their way toward him and Daisy.

"Soap," Jerome said.

"We have soap, and hot water, and a bed for you to sleep in and become well again," Daisy assured him.

He shook his head. "No, here." He reached into the pocket of his jacket and took out the hotel soaps that he had put there while in Berrin's room. "These have key impressions. One of them will match the apartment door of a dead girl." He pressed the bars into Daisy's hand. "Get them to Dare and Paula. She knows the dead girl. Berrin had her key. He killed her." He fumbled in his other pocket and produced the video tape that he had made in Schumann's hotel room. "Make sure that he sees this, too," he said. "He's a lawyer – he'll understand."

"We must tell the polizei," Daisy said.

Jerome shook his head. "Berrin's dead. He won't be back in the West." He straightened himself as well as he could and stepped back. "Daisy, you have got to go now."

"We will go," she said, stepping forward again. "Lean on me and we will be in the West in an hour. Perhaps less. A bus will stop just here in no more than a minute. From there we will go to the train and that will take us back to the West." She put her arm around him, her hand coming to rest on his jacket pocket. She pulled back as though burned.

"Why is it that you feel that you need a gun?" she asked. Her English was still tinged with Irish but the lilt was gone.

"It's the killer's. It will prove that Paula was framed."

"Then, I should take that, too?" She formed the words slowly, carefully.

Jerome shook his head. "You are taking too

many risks already. If you get caught with this I am going to have a whole new set of headaches."

"We have to go," she said.

He leaned down until they were at eye level. "Listen, and listen carefully. You have got to get through. If you are with me and they grab me – well, you have to get through."

"I don't want to go without you," Daisy said.

"Thank you," he answered. "But it has to be this way. You said that you would do what I asked."

Daisy seemed to steel her nerves and nodded once.

"Could I have," his voice was low, almost too low for her to be sure that she had heard him, "one kiss before you go?"

The tears broke and raced down her cheeks as she stepped into his arms, her face turned up and her lips welcomed his. She shook with silent sobs as they stood and held and kissed. Then he eased her away.

"Get out of here, kid" he said. "This is detective business." He brushed her cheek with the back of his hand and tried to smile. "And try not to look back, Daisy." He guided her around his body and gave her a gentle push to get her started. He resisted the temptation to watch her go. The two men were continuing their slow progress toward him when he heard the sound of air brakes. That would be the bus that Daisy had mentioned, he thought. He could hear the doors slide open in the still morning. Then they closed and he could hear the bus engine rev as it began to move on. He took his first steps forward.

The magpie called again. It looked at Jerome and then at the two men who approached steadily. Now it launched itself, banking toward the west and disappearing up a side alley.

The three men met in front of the bench that Daisy had slept upon. Jerome turned and sat without looking at the two men. After a few seconds the smaller man joined him on the bench.

"I've got a gun in my pocket," Jerome began. "That's not a threat. There aren't any bullets in it." He hoped that he would not have to prove that he was lying. It might give him an advantage if the man thought he was, essentially, unarmed. It would make it easier to shoot the two of them, if need be.

"So you have brought an empty weapon to a gun fight?" the man snickered. "You will forgive me if I do not offer to share."

"Not a problem. You see, this gun is going to prove that my friend is innocent of murder and that your boss isn't."

"I am afraid that I cannot allow this to happen," the man said. He shifted his weight and seemed about to stand.

"Hold on there, Rastus," Jerome said hastily.

"'Rastus'?" the man asked. "Who is this 'Rastus'? My name is Gerhardt."

"Well, that's great. But you mean you've never heard of 'Rufus Rastus Johnson Brown'?"

"Never. Who is this person and why should I care?"

"He's pretty famous where I come from. Rufus Rastus Johnson Brown – whatcha gonna do when the rent comes 'round? Whatcha gonna do – whatcha gonna say – whatcha gonna do on the Judgment Day?"

"You are stalling," Gerhardt said. "It is time for this to be finished." He stood and seemed to be loosening his shoulders before setting to work on Jerome again.

"Look," Jerome said, still trying to keep his voice smooth and gentle. "Your boss is dead." He glanced at Gerhardt out of the corner of his eye. The man seemed to be considering. "That's the truth. He's lying in a pool of his own blood up in those gardens."

"I do not believe you," Gerhardt said, but his voice indicated that he just might.

"How do you figure that I got his gun?" Jerome reasoned. Then, before the man could answer, he went on. "This whole operation is coming to a screeching halt. The NATO folks know it. The Kremlin folks know it. Even your boss knew it. So, unless you plan on finishing me off just for old time's sake, you are fresh out of reasons. Judgment Day is coming up on the calendar. You Stasi boys are going to have to do some pretty fancy footwork if you don't want to end up on the losing end of a gang fight with your own people."

"Own people?"

"You know – the ones that you've been terrorizing, torturing and killing – for their own good, of course, for the last forty years." Jerome's eyes flicked quickly to and from Gerhardt but the German was considering his words rather than looking at him.

"I can give you an hour," Jerome said. "After that…"

He didn't look up even when he knew that Gerhardt and his companion had walked away. The morning air was chill but the sun on his back felt good.

The magpie called from somewhere nearby. They can recognize themselves in a mirror, Jerome recalled. That was better than some people he had met.

*****

Gwendolyn Dean smiled as soon as she recognized Jerome. He returned the smile and cocked his head as if to say: 'Long time, no see,' though it hadn't been all that long. They had nodded to one another across the lobby of *The Colonnades* a half dozen times or more since he had returned from Germany. Once she had been with Huey and it was obvious to Jerome that she had seen him but was hoping that she hadn't been noticed. Jerome had pretended that he hadn't seen her and instead made a bigger-than-necessary production of commenting on the rain to the desk clerk while he closed his umbrella and put it in the stand. When he had looked around again she – and Huey – were gone.

"Good to see you," he said as they closed the distance between them.

Gwendolyn stopped in front of him at the "more than a friend, less than a lover" distance. "You, too! I heard you were working on a new book."

Jerome nodded and glanced around the lobby. He didn't see her boyfriend. "Yeah, it's coming along."

"You look good," she went on.

"Thanks, you, too." The emptiness of the conversation was beginning to wear on him already but he could tell that she wasn't through yet. She had made the effort to approach him. Overcoming the inertia was a major hurdle in itself. "How have you been?"

Gwendolyn's smile faded. "Lonely," she said. In

the instant that the word left her lips it seemed to surprise her as much as him. It was as though she had not planned to tell him but that the truth of the word could not be denied and it had asserted itself against her will. The word fell between them like a small pebble into a deep well. When it broke the surface it caused only a hollow sound and left no ripple.

Jerome's mouth opened but no words came out. He closed his lips and pressed them tightly together. He nodded once and sighed. "I'm very sorry to hear that," he said at last and she knew that he meant it. She also knew that he would not offer to try to change it.

They stood in awkward silence for a moment and then Jerome shuffled his feet as if to say: I have other things that I have to do, or, more honestly: I want to be somewhere that is not here.

He glanced over Gwendolyn's shoulder to the desk clerk, Martin, who was gesturing to him. Satisfied that he had secured Jerome's attention the clerk disappeared into the back office for a moment, reappearing with a florist's box. He stepped around the end of the counter and approached the two of them.

"Excuse me," Martin began, "These came for you while you were out."

Jerome nodded his head and took the box. A clear window of thin plastic displayed the flowers within. Daisies. "Yeah, Thanks, Martin," he said. Then, turning to Gwendolyn he tried to smile. "I ordered these. They're for someone. I, uh, I have to go," he said. "I'm meeting someone at the airport."

She forced a weak smile and bit her lower lip.

"I know you must get asked this all the time, but…" she reached into the bag slung over her shoulder and brought out a paperback. *When the Clock Strikes Dead* was blazoned across the top of the front cover and below that, in smaller, script: *A Jud Carson Mystery*. She held the book out to him. "Would you mind?"

"No, not at all," he answered. "Actually, I am very rarely asked to do this."

Then, for an instant they simply stood staring at one another. At last she reached out and took the flower box and he the book. He opened the cover and took a pen from his inside jacket pocket, thumbed it open and began to write.

"I liked it," she said when he had handed the book back to her and retrieved the flower box. "I guess that I'm going to have to collect all of your books now."

"I'm glad," he said. "And I am sure that my publisher will be, too."

Gwendolyn Dean forced a smile and took a deep breath. "It was good seeing you again," she said. "Take care."

Jerome nodded and turned, making his way across the lobby toward the entrance.

He didn't think about looking back.

Behind him the young woman opened the cover of the book that she held and read the neatly printed inscription:

"To Gwendolyn, I forgot to say that I always write from my own experience, one way or another. All the best," Below that was a scrawled signature.

*****

Excerpt, Daily Read File:
Saturday, 17 January 1990
BBC Monitoring/FBIS

(Berlin, FRG) In response to rumors that the GDR secret police have been destroying files rather than risk having their contents revealed, tens of thousands of Germans have stormed the organization's headquarters located on Normannen and Rusche streets. Ample evidence attests to the rumors substantiation.

Terrified guards opted to open the steel gates rather than be the targets of the masses who chanted such slogans as: Stasi to the mines, and, No pardon for the Stasi.

While the protesters initially were violent in their expressions toward the hated and feared secret police, calm did come to prevail and order was re-established. It should be noted that some few members of the crowd did manage to locate and read their own files, including some who learned that their own family members had spied on them for years.

It is expected that the revelations emerging from the Stasi headquarters will continue to affect the German culture for many years to come.

Chapter Sixteen

Notebook 24, Entry 27

"I don't know what happened to the letter that the third president of the United States supposedly wrote to or of his illicit love. I don't care. I had collared Stu Allgood and shanghaied him into getting Danny's briefcase from the pawn and taking it to Dixie. The note that I had sent along explained as much as I knew: there was a letter in the briefcase. It was probably worth a lot of money to presidential historians. If anybody deserved a break in this case it was Dixie LaBlanc for taking care of the man who had taken care of a lot of us.

"She kept her lip buttoned about it when every shamus in 'Frisco who had ever dipped a bill with Danny Granger paid his dues at the funeral.

"A week later I read that a woman named Audrey Paskill had been arrested and charged with Danny Granger's murder.

"Lt. Martinelli of the Homicide Squad had issued a statement that his department had acted on an anonymous telephone tip.

"Two columns over was a story about a man named Jeffrey Brighton who had been found dead in an abandoned car in the foothills. There was a torn piece of ivory colored paper still in his hand. I knew that I had come within an ace of being found in a car in the foothills.

"Still, I remember the taste of Elaine Merriman's kisses and the way that she made my heart race like a kid on a bike tearing down Telegraph Hill.

"Sometimes I still let her take my breath away."

When the Clock Strikes Dead
Jud Carson, P.I.

The End

About the Author:

John M. Spafford is a decorated former career Air Force intelligence analyst assigned to world-wide duties for the National Security Agency (NSA). After returning to civilian life, he took up his former occupation as a journalist and news photographer, culminating in his being named managing editor.

Mr. Spafford has earned his Paralegal certification, Bachelor of Arts degrees, *summa cum laude*, in psychology and in sociology, from the University of the State of New York, and Master of Arts from the University of Phoenix.

As a member of a forensic investigative team, Mr. Spafford brings his analytic skills to bear on criminal cases presented both pre-trial and post-conviction.

Mr. Spafford has taught at the college level and all levels of public education. He currently teaches high school subjects in a maximum security prison in Indiana.

A professional entertainer for more than twenty years, Mr. Spafford is an accomplished magician and singer-songwriter. He is a member of the National Writers Union (UAW Local 1981), the International Brotherhood of Magicians (I.B.M.) and the American Society of Composers, Authors and Publishers (ASCAP).

Thank You!

We hope that you have enjoyed this volume and would like to suggest that you consider the following titles:

Novels:

Sin in the Camp
The Legend of the Firedrake
Dead Duck & Gas Money
Reservoir Road

DVDs:

Electricity Comes to Winchester
Stand-up comedy by Ian A. Montgomery
recorded live in Winchester, Indiana

Albums:

Jean's Café Revisited
Original blues and folk-rock/alternative by
Ian A. Montgomery and featuring Rhiannon Spafford

To contact our authors/artists please direct your email
to:
BlueMaplePublishing@ymail.com